A
RAMSEY
WEDDING

BY
ALTONYA WASHINGTON

A RAMSEY WEDDING
Copyright © 2010 by AlTonya Washington

ISBN: 978-0-982978108

Printed in USA by CreateSpace

A week of chaos, desire, laughs and love…Ramsey style. Enjoy!

$\mathcal{ONE}$

Chicago, Illinois~ Sunday Evening…

"We can't do this now Ramsey." Contessa's warning ended on a gasp when she felt his tongue stab her someplace naughty, someplace intimate. Her hand weakened and it; along with the folder she'd held, slid to the bed.

"Can't do what?" Fernando teased while laughter touched the gravel depth of his voice.

"Stop talking…mmm…" she closed her eyes to savor the friction of his whiskered face grazing her thighs. "We've gotta get serious after this." She managed.

"Mmm hmm, stop talking," he countered and quickened the deep thrusts of his tongue.

An orgasm was imminent but Fernando chose not to help his fiancée get there just then. He ignored County's fist pounding his bicep. Instead, he eased up to pull her leg across his shoulder and took her in one smooth, lengthy stroke.

"Better?" He asked the question against her ear.

County murmured something senseless. Her fists now rested weakly against the stone wall that was his chest yet her hips bucked with a fire only he could douse. A hearty cry roused past her lips when he took a nipple and suckled harshly as he lunged.

Fernando raised his head as Contessa's cries gained volume. "Hush up, they'll hear you."

"Do you care?" County hissed.

"Hell no," his words were barely coherent. She was arching more breast into his mouth.

Eventually, sounds of lust and want overwhelmed them both filling the room with intensity while the couple achieved satisfaction in unison. Afterwards, it was the sound of heavy breathing filling the room as they lay sated.

"That the guest list?" Fernando cocked a brow toward the folder County had been holding.

"Mmm…" Her fingers grazed through the light brown curls covering his head. "I don't know why Mick's got me lookin' over this damn thing. All this is supposed to be her job."

"Aren't you the bride?" Fernando inquired and prepared to be hit.

County felt too relaxed for such action. "I gave Mick full control. All I want to do is walk down the aisle."

Fernando lifted his head. "To me," He grinned, the action sparking the adorable crinkles near his eyes. When she nodded, he leaned in to nuzzle her nose with his.

The kiss that began could have easily turned lusty, but Fernando pulled back. "You know you can't leave her hangin' that way." He took a love bite out of her shoulder. "Hop to it," he growled.

County kicked out her foot when he suddenly left the bed and headed to the bathroom. Smirking, she obeyed his orders and turned to her stomach to scan the list. Her brows drew close.

"Oh hell no!" She blared, taking all the covers with her when she scrambled from the bed.

Michaela's Chicago home would go on the market within a few weeks. County had insisted that her wedding be held there as the house was full of so many warm memories for Mick as well as herself.

Unfortunately, none of those warm and fuzzy thoughts were on Contessa's mind as she stormed down the long corridor to the room her soon-to-be ex best friend was sharing with her husband. As the wedding would be held there beneath a newly built gazebo at the end of the week; everyone decided to make a couple's retreat out of it. By Monday evening, the plan was to have the guest rooms accommodating six additional couples...including the newlyweds Kraven and Darby DeBurgh and Carlos and Dena McPhereson.

Just then however, County was imaging something more along the lines of a funeral than a wedding. She gave a quick booming knock to the door she'd approached and was already twisting the knob before she heard Mick's call to enter.

Michaela was tugging curls from the collar of her sweater. Her lips twitched when she took in the bed sheets twisted around County's otherwise nude body.

"Are you here to see me or Quest?"

Storming across the room, County held the open folder before Mick's face.

"Ah! The guest list you finished-"

Mick was reaching for the folder when County snatched it back and then held a single page closer to her face. "What's this?" She sneered.

"The guest list?" Mick answered carefully.

County rolled her eyes and pointed. "This?"

Again, Mick answered carefully. "Fernando's Aunt Willette from Georgia?"

County turned a bit so that she and Mick were both facing the page. She stabbed a finger against the name Neena Warren.

"Your...mom?" Mick braced herself to be hit.

"Right..." County breathed, lashes fluttering in phony satisfaction. "My mom- the only family I need. The only family I *expect* at my wedding. Now you tell me what the hell all these other bastards are doin' on the list?"

Before Mick could answer, the bathroom door opened. Quest stepped out- dark, to die for and dripping wet from his shower. He was only covered by a towel slung very low on his hips. Mick and County stared. For several moments the women totally forgot what they were discussing.

"This is awkward." Was all Quest could manage, wincing a bit as he spoke.

Michaela shrieked when County suddenly snapped to and dragged her from the bedroom.

In the hall, County pushed her friend against the wall. "Start talkin'."

Mick cleared her throat while pressing a hand to the base of her throat. "It was Miss Neena," she cleared her throat again when County's gaze narrowed. "Miss Neena told me to invite them."

"Say what?" County tilted her head in disbelief.

Mick nodded frantically. "I swear it. Miss Neena said she thought it'd be very gracious of you to invite your father and his side of the family." Mick delivered the last bit of info more softly.

Again, County's head tilted. "Are you trying to tell me you invited my entire family?"

Mick swallowed. "Everyone Miss Neena told me to. The ones on the list are all who've accepted so far."

County dropped her death grip on Mick's arm and turned to head back to her bedroom.

"Count?"

Dejectedly, Contessa only waved her hand and kept walking.

TWO

Monday...

Breakfast was en route to being a tense affair. Fernando and Quest had yet to be told why County was in such a foul mood. Michaela was filling the guys in when Contessa arrived in the kitchen.

"So tell me how you like your eggs," Quest asked, being the first brave soul to walk over and drape and arm around County's shoulder.

She worked on a smile, but failed. "Thanks Quest, I'll just have some juice."

"Hell no, you won't!" Fernando called across the kitchen.

"Ramsey..." County merely waved her hand.

"You need more than that."

"I don't."

"Contessa-"

"Alright, alright," she pressed fingers to her temples. "Whatever..."

Fernando shared looks with Quest and Mick. For County to give in so easily, meant she was truly rattled.

"Guess I'll have 'em scrambled, Quest."

"Talk to us, babe," Fernando urged, his striking gaze narrowed in concern.

"You already know it's about my family. I don't want 'em here." She took a seat at the table and watched them all gather around the kitchen island.

"That's it? You just don't want 'em here?"

County rolled her eyes away from Fernando, but didn't respond.

Fernando massaged his neck and tried to quell his temper. It didn't work. "We're getting married at the end of the week and I'll be damned if I watch you mope around for the better part of it."

She pounded a fist to the table and sent the silverware clattering. "I don't want my family- my father especially at my wedding, alright? Now Ramsey, I should think of all people *you* should be able to understand that!" Standing, she wiped her hands across the seat of her jeans and stomped from the kitchen.

Following the heated departure, Fernando and Quest looked to Mick for answers.

"Her dad and mom split up when she was about twelve or thirteen. She never told me why." Wearily, Mick took a seat at the island and shrugged. "I never asked her why."

"To hell with this," Fernando growled.

"Don't you think you should wait?" Mick asked when he was poised to push open the door.

"We're about to be married Mick." Fernando bowed his head as if he were contemplating. "She should at least be able to talk to *me*, right?"

Quest and Michaela shared a knowing smile and nodded.

County had gone off to the den and appeared engrossed in the movie she'd found. Fernando leaned against the jamb watching her for a minute or two. Last minute second thoughts had him moving away from the door before he recalled what he'd said to Quest and Mick.

"This is good," he called, smirking a bit when he noticed her jump at the sound of his voice. He took a seat next to her on the sofa. "Kim Basinger's character dies at the end."

Sighing heavily, Contessa rolled her eyes and clicked off the TV. "Thanks honey." Her voice was phony sweetness as she tossed the remote to the plaid armchair beside the sofa.

"Anytime," Fernando grinned and tugged up the sleeves of his Bears' sweatshirt. "So are you gonna tell me what'sup?"

"I just did."

"Count-"

"I can't talk to my father." Abruptly, she folded her arms across her chest. "I haven't talked to him in almost twenty years."

Fernando nodded, massaging his hands in an effort to resist pulling her close. "Mick said your folks split up when you were a kid. Was it ugly between them?"

County's laughter was long yet clearly forced. "*That's* a loaded question." She noted the confusion on his face and smiled. "It was ugly. It was *very* ugly."

"Will you tell me about it?"

"Baby I don't even like to *think* about it," she snapped back a curse and shook her head. "Talkin' about it ain't gonna happen."

"You might feel better." He tried but she'd moved over to straddle his lap then and words failed him.

"Since you've ruined the movie for me, you're gonna have to find some other way to entertain me." Leaning closer, she suckled his earlobe while grinding the soft bulge beneath his black sweats. "Lock the door," she murmured when the *bulge* gained definition.

Fernando cursed and pushed her away. Flopping back on the sofa, County pouted until she realized he'd gone to do as she asked.

***

"It's time to get past all that, Bunny."

County gripped the wood grain phone receiver and closed her eyes in agitation. County wasn't sure whether she was agitated by her mother's use of the childhood nickname or by the fact that the woman was so willing to forgive humiliation.

"Honey you know I'm right," Neena Warren's soft voice was even more soothing as she tried to calm her strong-willed daughter. "As for myself, I'm a few years shy of knocking on sixty's door and I've got no wishes to shadow the rest of my life with that petty crap."

"Mama how can you call it petty?"

"The point is that I can and if *I* can, can't you? He was my husband, Bunny. If I can let it go…"

Frustration warred with the need to do as her mother suggested. Viciously, she re-crossed her legs on the bedroom's window seat. "I don't think he ever knew how much he hurt us."

"Oh Bunny," Neena's laugh was more somber than amused, "trust me 'Hon, when you changed your last name to *my* maiden name, he knew."

County chewed her thumbnail for a second or three. "And what about the rest of his triflin' family?" She blurted as though their memory had almost escaped her.

"Dammit Contessa," Neena quietly murmured something about her only child driving her to drink and then asked the Lord to give her strength before she continued. "Listen to me everything's set for them to be there so just accept it. Forget about that past drama and focus on that sexy fiancé, soon-to-be husband of yours. I love you and I'll see you Friday." Neena hung up before her daughter could say another word.

***

The house grew livelier as the day progressed. The rest of the couples began to arrive in rapid succession. First in; around midday, were Quay and Ty. Quay's bad mood was apparent the instant he walked through the front door. At fault was his wife- at least that's the way Quaysar saw it. Tykira was wrapped up in a project she wanted to finish before the wedding. She scarcely said two words to anyone and headed right up to the room reserved for her and her husband.

Following a cursing tirade by Quay; once his wife had vanished, Michaela found a quiet corner. There, she prayed for a peaceful week amongst the eight hot-blooded couples soon to occupy the same roof.

The afternoon saw the arrival of everyone else including newlyweds Carlos and Dena McPhereson and Kraven and Darby DeBurgh. The house filled with calm beneath the business of unpacking and getting settled. By 5pm however, lunch and snacks had been thoroughly digested and the group collected in the kitchen to discuss dinner plans.

Johari and Nile were first to shoot down the idea of going out. Fernando and Quay suggested them cooking and were practically laughed out of the kitchen since everyone knew neither of them had intentions of lending their assistance in the area. Yohan suggested they draw names for kitchen duty. Of course, Melina celebrated her husband's brilliance until she discovered he had no intention of putting *his* name in for the drawing.

"It was my idea," was his excuse.

Once the names were drawn, Mel was again dismayed. Her name was selected along with Nile, Kraven and Moses.

Silence settled in the kitchen while the group mulled over the results. Because everyone else was thinking it, Nile slammed her hands to her sides and said, "This is going to be interesting."

"A Scotsman, a French damsel and two Americans…"

"Indeed," Kraven agreed with Moses' summation once the foursome stood alone in the kitchen having been charged with preparing a meal for sixteen adults.

"Anybody got any favorites?" Kraven inquired of his partners.

"Lots," Moses said enthusiastically before his dark gaze grew weary. "No idea how to make 'em, though."

Laughter rose slow but steady and shed a fair bit of the agitation.

Kraven rubbed his hands together and leaned next to Moses against the counter. "We need an entrée- a main dish."

"Right!" Mel snapped her fingers toward Kraven. "Have at it."

More laughter rumbled then, but Kraven graciously accepted the duty.

"Anyone have an idea to go with a dish for Salmon with Whiskey Sauce?" Kraven asked.

"Mmm…" Nile's lashes fluttered and she rubbed her hands across the Caribbean blue knit top she wore. "Mon Dieu, can't we just have that?"

Kraven slanted her a wink. "Nice try."

"Oh well, I call dessert." Nile went to check the fridge. "I make a pretty good Crepe Suzette."

"Go'on girl!" Melina and Moses cheered before joining Kraven and Nile in more laughter.

"Alright, alright," Mel began to wave her hands. "In that case, I can add a dish from half of my ethnic group and make Crab Rangoon for an appetizer."

"Impressive!" Kraven commended while checking the well-stocked cabinets. "We still need a side for my Salmon though."

Everyone looked to Moses who was already searching the pantry. They heard his cheer float from the area seconds before he emerged with a few cans in hand.

"I've got a recipe for baked potatoes and sauce." He checked the potato cupboard near the pantry and nodded. "Rub the sauce on the skin and it seeps through to flavor the meat of the potatoes." He said while checking the potato count.

Melina clapped. "I'd say the Scotsman, the French damsel and the two Americans have found their menu." She held out her hand for a group shake and waited for her partners to oblige before they all went to work.

"Hot damn! We're gonna be drunk just from dinner alone!" Carlos teased and smacked hands with Taurus while everyone else laughed and appreciatively eyed the spread.

Quest reached over to tug one of Mick's curls. "Watch it," he warned, ducking when she tossed her napkin at his face.

As Nile's Crepe Suzette contained a fair amount of Grand Marnier liquor and the Whiskey Sauce in Kraven's salmon contained its fair share of Scotch, the spirits ran high throughout the diverse menu.

"Alright y'all, dig in!" Moses announced when he arrived to set another bowl of sour cream to the table.

From then on, the dining room was silent but for murmurs to pass this or that and the clink of silverware to dinnerware.

During the meal, Quest noticed Ty had barely touched her food but she'd touched her sketch pad a plenty. He told her she could have her pick from a ton of rooms to work in.

"This place has more rooms that some castles I've seen." Quest told his sister-in- law.

Darby overheard. "I second that," she spoke around a mouth full of potatoes.

"Hey!" A wounded Kraven called down the table to his wife.

"Mick what the hell possessed you to buy such a big ass house?" Fernando questioned.

Mick shrugged, helping herself to more Salmon. "Never really thought about it. I'm such a pack rat." She handed the big fork to Dena who wanted another helping. "Anyway, all the rooms got used but never for what bedrooms are supposed to be used for." A devilish smile curved her mouth then. "I'm guessing that won't be the case this week."

"Damn right," Yohan agreed.

The room roared with laughter.

When dinner was done and the kitchen set to rights, everyone ventured off to various parts of the house to enjoy the remainder of the evening.

Michaela caught up to County who was heading upstairs.

"Hey?" Mick tugged her friend's sleeve before she'd gotten too far ahead. "I'm very sorry for not clearing the family issue with you first."

County smiled but said nothing as she reclined against the banister.

"It's just um…with all my *issues* with family, I just figured it important that they be here." Easing both hands into the back pockets of her Capri jeans, Mick shrugged. "Knowing them, keeping *some* communication open, it's important, you know?"

"It's fine," County leaned over to pull her into a hug.

"You're sure?" Mick snuggled into the embrace.

County had to laugh when she nodded. "I just can't believe how cool Mama's being about it all- after the way he left."

Mick pulled back from the hug. "Maybe she's trying to focus on the future- stomp out the crap in her past and all that progressive stuff?"

"I guess." County nodded.

Mick lifted a shoulder. "Maybe you could try some of that progressive stuff too, hmm?"

County managed a half smile and tugged Mick into another hug.

THREE

Tuesday...

The morning held a special glee that went without saying. Quest and Mick would celebrate three years of marriage that day. With all that had occurred between the couple just months earlier, the celebration held an even more special meaning.

Breakfast duties went to Quest, Yohan, Taurus and Johari. By the time the group had assembled, the cooks had prepared a feast of grits with steak strips and gravy, mounds of scrambled eggs, cinnamon toast, fruit and cheese.

Mick was last down the stairs; and the only one to hear the doorbell over all the conversation and laughter filtering throughout the kitchen. When she opened the front door, her mouth fell open and could have easily reached the checkered floor of the foyer. She just managed to pat the backs of the two women who pulled her into a double hug.

"Hey girl, it's us," one of the women said when she pulled back from the hug and mistook Mick's surprise for confusion.

"Monique and Trenique Samuels- Conty's cousins," The other woman supplied.

"Of course, of course," Mick began to nod.

"We just *had* to come by and see where Conty was getting married." Trenique said, already peeking beyond Michaela's shoulder with unmasked interest.

"And since we live so close and all…" Monique absently toyed with the heavy gold chain around her neck while observing the lofty ceiling. "It's a shame we all lived in Chi-town once and hardly saw each other." She went on while her sister headed beyond the foyer.

"Where is Conty, Mick?" Trenique was asking while staring dazedly at a lovely oil painting near the den.

Michaela snapped to and led the way. The sisters talked the entire time complimenting the house, the furnishings, even Mick's hair and outfit. For all their loud talk and laughter however, the two women turned dead silent upon stepping to the kitchen and spotting the heavenly assemblage of male magnificence filling the space.

Trenique made some non-descript sound of awe while her sister swallowed…with effort.

"Good Lord," Monique eventually breathed.

Mick understood their disbelief and was thankful it had quieted their rambling. Conversation in the kitchen quieted as well, giving Mick the chance to make a blanket introduction.

County emerged through the crowd. Her eyes were filled with the same disbelief that Mick's had been moments earlier.

Fernando moved forward too and was extending a hand toward his fiancées' cousins. "Ladies," he greeted.

Of course, Monique and Trenique were floored but that didn't stop them from giggling like school girls or thrusting out ample sized chests-as if that were necessary given the shamefully tight sweaters they wore with equally tight jeans.

"Can we offer you breakfast? We've got plenty." Fernando asked once the ladies were idled up next to him.

"They can't stay." County announced even as Trenique was nodding yes.

"Ooooh, we're so happy for you girl," Monique was saying as she pulled her cousin into a hug.

"What the hell are y'all doin' here?"

Monique pulled out of the hug. She continued to smile, though it was apparent that her cousin's blatant mood was wearing through her calm.

"Well it didn't make sense not to drop over and speak." The faintest tinge of laughter held to Monique's voice. "Not with us all being right here in Chicago and everything."

"Bullshit. This is the first time y'all ever *dropped over* to see me, so cut it."

Conversation and eating had resumed once the introductions were made. That all ceased once County snapped.

Fernando's translucent stare narrowed in surprise. "Contessa," his head tilted slightly when he spoke her name softly.

Trenique waved a hand. "Don't bother Fernando. We should've known this bitch hadn't changed."

County's smile was pure delight. "Not a bit, so why the hell are y'all here?"

Monique was practically snarling. "At least you finally got some decent friends Conty. If it wasn't for Mick we probably wouldn't even have gotten an invite."

"There's no 'probably' about that Mony." County propped a hand to her hip. "And Mick was only doing what she was told. Mama asked her to invite your jackass family. I coulda done without seein' any of you bastards."

"County," Michaela moved closer to her friend then.

"Conty you still the same stank actin' stuck up bitch you always were!" Monique hissed before she was pushed aside by her sister.

"Just cause you done hooked up with society, don't forget we knew you when you was wearin' *our* hand-me-downs." Trenique raged.

"And your Mama was bummin' food stamps off ours!" Monique chimed in.

Trenique nodded. "You come from the same hood we do, skank."

"Mmm hmm," County folded her arms over her yellow pleated tube blouse. "*Unlike* you, I'm not there any more."

Ready for blows, Trenique jerked forward. "Bitch, I got a place on the lake so fuck you!"

County was not impressed. "It's a state of mind Tren and how many dicks did you have to suck to get that place on the lake?"

Fernando was there to restrain both sisters, while Mick held onto Contessa.

"We shoulda known this was gonna be the same old shit from you Conty!" Monique cried.

Contessa however was quite calm. "I guess that means y'all won't be coming to the wedding then?" She made sure they heard the hope in her voice.

Monique rolled her eyes. "Come on Trenne let's get the hell out of here!"

The women stormed out of the kitchen but Mick held onto County for good measure. The front door slammed and the sound seemed to vibrate throughout the now silent house.

County wrenched out of Mick's hold and stomped up the back stairway.

"Fuck this," Fernando growled, preparing to go after her.

"That might not be the best idea, mate." Kraven advised.

"I gotta agree with that." Moses said from his position near the fridge.

Fernando massaged his neck, and then whirled around. "Mick what the hell is all this?"

"Damned if I know." Mick sounded just as lost and puffed out her cheeks as she leaned against the kitchen island. "She never talked a lot about her family, I only met 'em a few times and that was if we went out and happened to see 'em somewhere." She began to massage her arms through the peach scoop necked sweater she wore. "County was always cool about it- making intros, small talk…maybe this visit was just a bit too unexpected."

She met Fernando's questioning gaze. "Guess she didn't have time to put on her mask."

He grimaced as understanding fell into place. The jovial mood that started the day was irrevocably marred and breakfast passed in virtual silence.

***

Half an hour or so after breakfast ended, Fernando was making his way up to his and County's room.

"Fern?"

About to take the second floor landing, Fernando stopped, turned and smiled. "Here to warn me again?" he teased.

"Nah," Kraven grinned. "As mad as she was earlier, she may've killed you. She's probably over it now."

Fernando laughed. "You don't know my fiancée very well. You'll want to eat those words by the end of the week."

Kraven shrugged. "I doubt that. By week's end she'll be looking forward to her honeymoon someplace with an incredible sunset."

"Mmm yeah, that does sound good right about now."

"Speaking of incredible sunsets, my wife has a very interesting painting in her possession."

Fernando's confusion was evident.

"Reminds me of the place where you and I first met." Kraven folded his arms across the faded replica of the Scottish flag that adorned his T-shirt. "A certain little island getaway when we were all lads…"

Understanding flooded Fernando's light eyes. "You sure it's the same place?"

"It's no map," Kraven glanced across his shoulder, "but I'd know that strip of beach anywhere. Only someone else who'd been there could have drawn it."

Fernando stroked the whiskers covering his jaw and looked off into the distance. "How'd Darby get it?"

"Some woman," Kraven sighed and leaned against the banister. "She didn't give a name, but from my wife's description, it sounded just like Persephone."

Fernando stood straighter. "Persephone James? Have you told Hill?"

"There's more." Kraven said as he nodded. "Talk of a clean-up project."

The phrase had Fernando leaning against the banister as well. The clean-up projects; and what they involved, were when the young men running away to fun and irresponsibility finally realized what would be expected of them.

"Are you serious?" Fernando breathed, bumps raised along his chilled skin.

"I wish I wasn't, mate but it appears Hill's info is prime," Kraven shrugged. "It makes sense, you know?"

"Does Taurus know?"

Kraven grimaced. "He suspects things, but knows I'll tell him when the time is right."

"My family can't handle anymore shit, Kray."

"I don't think it'll come to that, mate."

"Hell, I'm not talkin' about my family under this very roof."

"I thought those ties were broken?" Kraven straightened a bit from his leaning stance. "Sabella and Pike are divorced; Sabra and Smoak hate each other and Bill…"

"Exactly," Fernando turned and squeezed his hands around the banister. "They've each got ties to that family that could easily become relevant again."

Kraven turned as well. "You really think that has a chance of happening?"

"Before Yohan and Melina got back together and Moses and Johari found each other again- I'd have said hell no, but corny as it may sound- love finds a way."

"Will you ever tell Contessa all of what happened back then?" Kraven's voice sounded hushed.

"All?" Fernando smirked. "Never. You? Will you share it with Darby?"

Kraven raked a hand through his dark hair. "Never all-a good bit though, when she's had one of my babies and is pregnant with the next." He slanted Fernando a sly wink. "We should have a

talk with your family then?" He asked once their chuckles had
subsided.

Fernando sighed. "Indeed."

***

Following the upset that rocked the morning, everyone
relished the quiet and uneventful-ness of the day. A vicious rain
down poured just before lunch and added to the somber mood of
the afternoon.

Quay bit his lip and watched Tykira still hard at work in
their room. When her pencil slowed and she bit on the eraser, he
knocked once on the doorjamb.

"Can I have a minute?"

Concern filled her almond shaped gaze and she dropped the
pencil. "Are the guys okay?"

"Yeah," Quay waved a hand, "yeah, their fine- probably
feelin' like little kings with all that spoiling my folks and Miss
Bobbie are layin' on them and Quinn."

Ty laughed while reaching for her pencil.

Quay braced off the jamb and moved further into the room.
"Just wanted to know if you were eating lunch," he toyed with the
ponytail that flounced to the middle of her olive green T-shirt.

"Mmm...I don't think so," she was reverently studying the
pad and only murmured the absent reply.

It was Quay's turn to be concerned and the emotion
mirrored in the onyx depth of his gaze. "You hardly touched your
breakfast or even dinner last night." He reminded her softly despite
the fact that her weird mood was stroking his temper to frenzy.

Ty was smiling. "In all fairness Quay, I don't think
anybody much had their minds on breakfast."

Quay's grin sparked his right dimple. "Amen." He recalled
that morning's dramatic events. "So I guess that's a no on lunch?"
He took note of her set expression.

"Sweetie, I'm sorry," Ty sighed and tugged on the side of
his saggy jeans. "It's just these projects I'm trying to finish."

"Smoak's stuff?" He guessed.

"Yeah," she reached for his hand while she spoke. "Still no specifications on the locale or anything," she kissed the back of his hand. "How 'bout I have half of whatever you're having?"

"Works for me," he leaned close. "Gimme some," he ordered, cupping her chin while tilting her head up for his kiss. The lazy strokes of her tongue against his had Quay seconds from dragging her to their unmade bed. Reluctantly, he pulled back and she dived into more sketching. The concern never left his dark stare.

No lights burned in the suite shared by Mr. and Mrs. Carlos and Dena McPhereson. The couple didn't mind for they preferred to relish their solitude snuggled on the room's massive bed which was situated before the French doors. The doors were open and revealed the pelting rain that drenched the ground and the wrought iron railing surrounding the brick balcony.

Dena sighed and smiled when Carlos hugged her tighter.

"Bored?" His clear deep voice filled the room.

"Not even…" she almost purred.

"Mmm…"

A playful frown marred Dena's dark lovely face. "Do you want me to be?" She laughed.

"No," Carlos kept hold of her while angling his muscular frame into a more comfortable position. "But if you *were* bored, it'd give me the chance to use my male wiles to entertain you."

Dena's resulting giggle was a mix of happiness and wickedness. "You know you can use your *wiles* on me regardless of my mood."

A delicious kiss followed. Carlos lost his hands in his wife's gorgeous bouncy locks and shivered at the mere feel of her in his arms. In spite of his satisfaction it didn't stop him from reading her expression when he pulled back. "Don't try convincing me something heavy isn't on your mind, De."

"It's not *heavy*, it's not." She swore when his ruggedly handsome features tightened. "Just what happened with County's family this morning…makes me wonder if you've stopped to ask yourself what becoming part of my family means?" She gave a one shoulder shrug that nudged the strap of her black cami. "You and Sheila are from a pretty quiet, normal bunch." She referred to Carlos' sister.

"Yep," he lay on his back and tapped a hand to his chest. "Our lives were pretty uneventful before we knew you Ramseys."

Dena shifted and looked down at him. "The things that brought us back together were pretty eventful." Her eyes fell to the wide band around his ring finger. "We were so caught up in the past and all that happened, we didn't stop to think of the now and the future."

Sleek brows closed over Carlos' deep set eyes. "What are you trying to say, De?"

"I swear I love you." She vowed without hesitation before her expression turned uneasy again. "It's just that right now things in my family are almost fairy-tale like with all the love and happiness floating around...such things rarely last long in my family- you know this."

"I know," he wished the brush of his hand across her cheek could remove the sadness from her face. "And I'd probably take what you just said as gospel except for the fact that during all our ups and downs, through all the nastiness...one thing lasted- our love." He curved his thumb around the alluring tilt of her mouth. "Had it not lasted, we wouldn't be married now, right?"

Dena contemplated his words but for a second. Like a fog lifting, her expression suddenly brightened. She blinked as though his words had revealed some truth that had been right before her eyes.

"See?" He spotted her spirits lifting.

"I swear I love you." She whispered in a much happier tone before she captured his mouth in a searing kiss.

Carlos growled and flipped Dena to her back where the moment grew more heated.

Darby was dropping a frilly lingerie piece into an overnight bag when two steel bands encircled her waist.

Kraven propped his chin on her shoulder and peeked over into the case. "That for me?"

"No," she laughed and hid the piece beneath a ratty old T-shirt. "As I recall you prefer to see me *out* of my clothes."

"Ah, you're correct Lady DeBurgh." He whispered and reached beneath her pearl blue hoody to undo her bra.

"Stop!" She ordered playfully while shifting out of reach from his nimble fingers. "We don't have time and as I also recall you like your love scenes lengthy."

Kraven's rich laughter filled the room them. "As you *recall*? Well now I've got to do something to keep my love scenes at the forefront of your mind, lass."

"Kraven...Kraven no...No!" She shrieked when his merciless tickling began. "Come on now please- I need to get this stuff packed. We're leaving for Vegas tomorrow, remember?" She said referring to the bachelorette and bachelor parties for the bride and groom at Sabra's casino resort.

"Besides," she changed gears then and pushed her husband to their bed. "I was wondering when you might tell me the truth about that painting of mine."

Kraven's grimace narrowed his jade stare. "I thought that might have to be the one secret between us as man and wife?" He asked in a hopeful tone before his expression dimmed. "It's not my fondest memory. More like a nightmare."

Darby sat astride him. "About those islands in Scotland? The boys you met there?"

"Partly. All this happened later."

She fiddled with the heavy silver buckle of his belt. "You met Fernando there?"

"Aye, knew him long before his cousin." He was referring to Taurus then and smiled. The gesture faded though as memories returned of the horrors he and Fernando Ramsey witnessed as boys.

When his vibrant greens clouded over, Darby knew. "You aren't gonna tell me, are you?"

"Sorry love," he pressed a ragged kiss into her palm. "In time, but for now it's best this way." He tugged her down to lie prone against him. "Do you trust me?"

"With my life, Lord DeBurgh," she vowed and then proved it in the strength of her kiss.

"Is that romantic, or what?" Johari tucked a wayward sandy red lock behind her ear and hugged herself. She and Melina were chatting and found their way into the sitting room. There, they caught sight of Taurus and Nile outside on the patio. The couple slow danced in the rain to a melody only they could hear.

"Exquisitely romantic," Mel agreed, sharing the arm of the chair her cousin occupied. "Think we could persuade the guys to do that?"

Johari's silver stare narrowed wickedly. "I did with Moses well...almost...the rain caught us outside while we were arguing."

Melina burst into laughter and Jo couldn't help but follow suit.

"So what about Yohan?"

"Mmm..." Mel waved a hand. "Once you've made love in a weight room...little else comes close." She shrugged and glimpsed her cousin watching her in awe.

"I do believe I'm offended." Jo toyed with the back tie of her striped tee. "I haven't been privy to the details of that little escapade."

Mel bumped her shoulder. "Not sure those are details you can handle."

Simultaneous laughter erupted before the somberness set in.

"Dammit," Johari cursed and blinked back sudden tears, "I wish Zara could have had just a little of this- just a little before..."

"Shh..." Mel turned fully and enveloped Johari in hug. "It wasn't fair- not a damn bit of it, but somehow...somehow it all had to happen just the way it did."

"I know," Johari sniffled in a somewhat refreshing manner. "Doesn't mean I have to understand it, you know?"

Melina kissed the top of her head. "I know."

The two were still hugging when their husbands found them and hustled them out onto the rainy patio to share the dance space with Nile and Taurus.

***

Michaela was seated before her bathroom vanity, fresh from a shower and applying lotion to her face and neck when she looked up and saw Quest through the mirror.

"Some anniversary, huh Mr. Ramsey?"

He pushed off the doorjamb and closed the distance between them. "Aren't they all?" He asked, throwing a leg across the overstuffed seat she occupied and settling down behind her.

"Complaints?"

"Not a one."

"Ah, come on, you can tell me." She reached for the lotion again only to have him hold it out of her reach.

"Not a one," he said when her amber gaze met his gray one in the mirror.

Michaela gave a little shrug. "There've been some not so good times in there."

Quest bowed his head, trailing his nose along her shoulder. "Without them we wouldn't be as strong as we are." He murmured into her bare skin.

Mick gave a saucy toss of her head. "We are kinda strong, aren't we?"

"Damn strong." He took the lotion and set about massaging the creation into her shoulders.

Mick leaned back when his hands moved in front to work the lotion into her breasts and stomach. She linked an arm up and around his neck. "So tell me, what does a captain of industry such as yourself, do for his wife to celebrate three years of wedded bliss?"

"Hmm…" Quest set the lotion to the vanity and pretended to concentrate. "Let's see…with a house full of black folk-"

"And one Scotsman."

"Right," the left dimple flashed when he grinned. "A house full of folk- hungry, rained in and agitated by the day's events… order pizza and get drunk of course."

Mick giggled so hysterically, she tumbled right off the seat and landed on her bare bottom.

"I love it!" She cried while her husband simply laughed at her.

FOUR

Wednesday~ Las Vegas...

Parties were the order of the day-or rather evening and pre-dawn. The group traded their Chicago digs for the flash and dazzle of the Vegas realm.

Sabra stood atop the roof of her first tower and watched her cousins and their wives exit the choppers that had carried them from the jet strip to her hotel.

"Thing of beauty," she sighed, one hand in the pocket of her almond brown cargo Capris, the other at her brow to visor the beaming late afternoon sun. She refused to acknowledge the slight wrench of her heart whilst she took in the blatant love and desire that was almost tangible between each of the eight couples. The bride and groom were first to approach and envelop her in hugs.

"Congratulations!" Sabra called over the whipping wind courtesy of the helicopters.

"Are you sure you can't come back with us for the wedding? Just for the day?!" County used her purse as a visor against the sun while yelling the question.

Sabra was already shaking her head. "Sorry girl, but I'm expecting a group of record label execs and their clients!" She shrugged. "I like to be on hand for those arrivals-let them fools know I don't tolerate no shit on my premises!"

"My cousin the watchdog!" Fernando laughed and kissed her cheek.

Sabra brushed him off and waved to the rest of the group. "There's a buffet spread!-" She rolled her eyes toward the choppers when they finally slowed and silenced the air about them. "There's a late lunch waiting in your suites." She spoke while accepting hugs and kisses from her guests.

"Everything's all set for your parties." She grinned at Fernando and Contessa then turned to the two men and three women in uniform. "These folk will be on hand to see to anything else you may need."

"Pretty classy, girl," Quay was saying. "I'd have never expected all this from you." He winked.

The group burst into laughter when Sabra tapped her bottom once in a silent request for her cousin to kiss it. Everyone dispersed soon after and Tykira walked on ahead with Sabra.

"Are you sure about not coming back with us?" Ty asked. "Looks like everyone's gonna be there."

"No offense Ty," Sabra let down some of the happy guard she'd erected, "watching all of you in love and lust for one night's gonna be more than enough for me."

Ty took Sabra's elbow, stopping their stroll from the rooftop. "How long will you let him get you down like this? The two of you aren't even in the same state for cryin' out loud."

"Sometimes I just get the feeling that it's not all finished between us." Sabra's head tilted when she glimpsed something in Ty's mahogany stare. "What?" She probed, stepping closer. Even when Tykira shook her head, she studied her for a few additional moments before they followed everyone else inside.

***

"Whoo Hoo!" Contessa pressed a hard kiss to her fiancés' cheek when he turned his head and grinned back at her.

Shortly after settling into their suite at Sabra's, Fernando asked County to accompany him. The last thing she expected was for him to whisk her away on a motorcycle for a ride across the Mojave.

The sun, not quite as potent just then, combined with the wind hitting her face. It lifted her clipped locks and was like a dash of freedom that coursed over her body and washed away the agitation of the last few days.

"Not that I'm complaining Ramsey, but what the hell possessed you to do this?" County was asking once they'd left the bike to take up residence on a towering boulder. From there, the plan was to enjoy a glorious desert sunset.

Fernando reclined on the rolled sleeping bag he'd packed and pulled County down to him.

"Thought you could use the time away," he pulled off his sunglasses and set them in the gloves placed next to a knapsack.

Content then, she snuggled into his massive frame and she was quiet for a while. "You want the real story on my family, don't you?" She asked later.

"Absolutely," he shrugged, "but who am I to badger you about giving it to me?"

County sat up, wincing when she pulled away her shades to perch them atop her head. "The Warrens are nothing like the Ramseys."

"And the Samuels?"

"Bunch of hood rats," County blurted in reference to her father's family. "Shit," she cursed her loss of control and then smiled. "My mom had two sisters- very normal, very wonderful and with wonderfully boring lives led with two of the best uncles a girl could have. They all live in Virginia." She squinted out over the unending expanse of the sparse and lovely desert.

"Nice lives," she sighed and drew up her legs to rest her chin on jean clad knees. "Only dark clouds were that neither could have kids. My mom was the lucky one there and dammit all if she didn't have to land the sorriest sperm donor in the world."

"Ouch," Fernando whispered when she looked back at him.

County looked back toward the view. "I didn't know he was sorry- like all little girls, I loved my dad and he treated me like- like a princess." She blinked suddenly feeling unexpected tears pressuring her eyes. "Yeah, daddy treated me like a princess but his family…"

"The hood rats," Fernando teasingly supplied.

"Sorry bunch of bastards," She shook her head. "Do you know they've *never* had a reunion? No kind of get together as a family. Reason? Because *this* person wouldn't come if *that* person was gonna be there."

"It's not exclusive baby," Fernando's laughter echoed. "Same crap happens in my family all the time."

"Yeah, but you've never had to live with slutty, skanks-ville cousins." County pulled the sunglasses from her head and toyed with them. "When my dad…walked out, my mom was stranded in Chicago. She was stranded and proud. Wouldn't even call her sisters but that was okay 'cause we lived off the good graces of the Samuels. I tried to tell her *that* was a bad move but she wasn't hearin' it." She muttered a curse and threw a pebble over the side of the boulder.

"Those bitches…my dad's sisters with their roach infested houses and trick ass daughters-men traipsin' in and out all day and fuckin' night and they had the nerve to make me and Mama feel lower than dirt. And didn't bother to talk behind Mama's back either, told my mom straight out that it was her fault Daddy left…"

Fernando ignored his temper rising over what she'd been forced to live through. He pulled County back to lie against him, keeping his arms tight about her.

"I'd have lived on the street rather than stay there; I hate 'em- all of 'em." She bristled. "Everything I've accomplished- all I have…it's been about me gaining distance- physical, emotional, you name it. I swore no one would ever make me or my mom feel like less. Ever again." She didn't bother to blink back tears then. "Seeing those two bitches the other morning took me right back to those days." She shook her head against his chest. "I don't want to know that life anymore, Ramsey."

She broke then. Hard. Fernando didn't try to shush or soothe knowing she'd be all the better for it when she was spent.

"I didn't miss it." County sighed when she next opened her eyes to find that the sun hadn't set. She tuned in to the feel of lips caressing her temple. Then she noticed her clothes were missing.

"Ramsey?" She queried, finding him as nude as she was inside the sleeping bag they shared.

The smile sent his eyes to crinkling. "Come on now, you know I couldn't let all this beauty go to waste."

"The sunset?"

"That's beautiful too."

"I love you Fernando."

"And I love you." He spoke into her mouth as he kissed her.

As everything between them tended to turn hot and lusty in the span of a second, this kiss was different. It was a kiss of emotion and promise which sparked a unique heat all its own. Fernando made love to her with his mouth first, allowing it to be the only part of his body to touch her.

Hands braced on the thickness of the gray and black bag, his lips traced the line of her neck, and his tongue darted out to take a dip in the hollow at the base of her throat before traveling her collarbone. He squeezed his eyes shut, urging himself to go slow when she arched up and murmured his name.

While Fernando only allowed his mouth permission to touch, Contessa wasn't so stingy. Her hands were everywhere traveling the awesome expanse of his chest which glistened a deep shade of caramel against the vibrant blaze of the setting sun. She bit her lip at the intimidating width of his powerful arms; muscles bulging with his hands fisted on either side of her and struggling not to touch.

"Please," she was shameless when her fingers grazed the orgasm-inducing length of his erection. He resisted when she tried to draw him down.

Instead, his mouth continued its journey and he added his nose to the trip outlining the seductive curve of her bosom. His tongue mimicked the outlining by paying special attention to her nipples. He manipulated one between his teeth then suckled harshly until the tip was rock solid and glistened wet amidst rays of the sun.

County bit her lip but couldn't silence the trembling cry that escaped into the atmosphere and reverberated around them. Fernando's head disappeared along with the rest of him. He finally added his hands to the mix when she arched against his mouth as he tongued her navel. Big hands steadied her hips and allowed him to have his way.

Being tickled and aroused at the same time, the sounds County uttered then were a mix of humor and yearning. She raked her fingers through the silky brown curls covering Fernando's bowed head. His nose nudged the folds of her center and he gave her hips a warning squeeze when she tried to move.

Contessa's hands slid from his hair to cover his hands where they gripped her hips. She tried to pull them away and succeeded only to have him move to grip her thighs. She uttered a trembling moan when his tongue was inside her. What she wanted was *him* inside her.

"Ramsey please, you don't have to-"

"You trying to tell me how to do this?" He growled in the midst of feasting on her body.

"Mmm..." she shook incessantly. "No, no I'm not but-"

"Then shut up," his thumbs massaged her clit while he drove his tongue deeper.

He proceeded to stroke her out of her mind. Contessa didn't care how grandly she fed his ego then; he'd pushed her too far to give a damn. She cried out into the shaded desert confessing to the rocks, dirt, brush and wildlife how incredible he was.

She took what he gave until he finished and rose above to grant her the privileged of suckling her essence from his tongue. The eagerness of her kiss broke down whatever resistance he had left and gave County the chance to turn the tables. She pushed him to his back and tortured him just as he'd done to her. She suckled his nipples, capturing his wrists and trapping them above his head when he tried to resist. When he begged her to stop, she grinned.

"Trying to tell me how to do this, Ramsey?"

His laughter sounded breathless. "County-"

"Shut up." Her tongue glided down then, paying tribute to the striking array of muscles that appeared carved into his abdomen. Her nails grazed his sides and the powerful line of his thighs.

"Contessa…" he groaned when her mouth sheathed his shaft. "Dammit wait." He made no move to stop her.

As he'd done earlier, County brought her hands down on his hips to stop their movement. She moaned while sliding her lips along his rigid length. A wave of arrogance caused her to shiver when he confessed the excellence of her oral skills to the environment.

Dangerously close to coming then, he reclaimed control and dragged her up and over him. Settling her beautifully to his moist, throbbing stiffness he directed the lift and rotation of her hips.

County felt weak and exhilarated at once. The dessert breeze blew comfortably across her skin and through her hair. She had no control of her actions which suited her fine. Fernando's big hands cupped her bottom, at times pulling her off his cock when release was at hand. Shameless, she begged him to come inside her.

Fernando didn't want to, not when he was being ridden so exquisitely by the beauty astride him. Being pleasured by an exquisite beauty had its price though and he couldn't ignore the demands of his body for long. Flipping her to her back then, he nibbled on the tip of a bouncing breast and took her with a savagery that had them both crying out into the evening. They came simultaneously atop the boulder in the Mojave.

***

Had the topic of conversation not been so remorse, Fernando could have easily given himself a pat on the back for being mature enough to forego the customary bachelor party-complete with a never ending bar, strippers, the works…

Unfortunately, the chances were slim of getting together this particular group and in such a spot where chances of them being disturbed were low and weren't likely to come round again. Besides, it was past time for his brothers and cousins to know more- a *bit* more about how he'd spent those...dangerous years of his life.

Still; as it was a bachelor party, an abundance of drinks and toasts were in order. More than a few rounds of bellowing laughter roared from the table, but no one complained.

Sabra's Lair was aptly named. Aside from the dark, gothic appeal of the furnishings and colors, the place attracted the bulk of the hotel's male patronage. The waitresses were model-lovely and discreet, though the same could not be said for their uniforms. Satiny bra-styled tops, bare midriffs and black tap pants were the order of dress in the Lair. Not surprising, the lovely servers drew impressive tips and even more numbers. On that score, Sabra's policy was strictly: *don't ask, don't tell.*

Not surprising, the ladies made several trips to the Ramsey/DeBurgh/McPhereson table that evening. Most times, it was simply to ask if anyone needed extra napkins, or fresh drinks.

The guys were all polite and never sounded agitated over the abundance of interruptions as their conversation gained momentum. Sabra's employees however, were well-trained and knew when enough was enough. As the conversation gained momentum, it turned the faces of the eight gods occupying the secluded back table, to guarded tense masks. Regardless of how magnificent the men were to look at, the waitresses knew the goings on at the table weren't open to interruptions- well meaning or otherwise.

"No offense Krave but...a painting?" Taurus' skepticism was etched perfectly on his face. "How do you guys know the painter wasn't just copying something they'd seen?"

"Right," Yohan chimed in while swirling the ice in his bourbon. "It's possible whoever painted the damn thing didn't know what they were looking at."

Kraven exchanged a look with Fernando before he nodded. "I'd agree if it weren't for the description Darby gave of the woman who donated it to the studio. I'd bet everything it was Persephone James."

"And what's she got to do with it?" Quay asked.

Kraven shrugged. "She and Hill…"

No further explanation was needed on that point. The rest of the guys bowed their heads.

"So exactly what are y'all trying to tell us and why does it matter that Persephone gave Darby this painting?" Carlos inquired.

Again, Kraven and Fernando slanting meaningful looks across the table.

"Do y'all remember when I ran away?" Fernando spoke up then.

The group chuckled as memories resurfaced.

"Mama couldn't eat for weeks," Yohan recalled. "She was skinny as a stick by the time the P.I. Marc hired found you tryin' to make your way back."

"Yeah, I was desperate to get back by then." Fernando rubbed his fingers through his hair and leaned back in the cushioned armchair he occupied at the table. "Even life with Marc Ramsey seemed like Disneyland compared to…"

"Compared to what?" Quest leaned over to lay a hand across his cousin's.

Fernando turned his hand over to squeeze Quest's. The contact seemed to give him strength to continue. "I was looking for a place to be understood." He looked over at his brother. "You know what I mean, Mo."

Moses' dark gaze narrowed in understanding. "You didn't?" He whispered, stunned. "You didn't really go there?"

Quaysar studied his cousins, and then leaned close to Carlos. "Why do I feel like we're the only ones who don't know the punch line of this story?"

"Could you guys get to the point?" Quest encouraged.

Moses rolled his eyes away from Fernando. "Y'all know that me and Hill became friends through a mutual acquaintance?"

"Right," Everyone spoke in unison.

"Mama didn't like him." Yohan remembered.

"Which made me like him even more. I met Gram Walters long before Hill though. The guy came from a background a lot like ours but without the dollars." Moses smoothed a hand over his shaved head. "His mother didn't give a damn about him, father wasn't worth shit...all the guy ever talked about was getting away- talked about it all the time but he was smart enough to know he didn't want to live on the streets." Moses took a swallow of his gin.

"One day he comes talkin' about some organization." Moses grinned. "I didn't know the cat could spell, let alone pronounce a word like that...anyway, he'd met some older guy who'd talked his ear off about this *organization*. It was open to young men- an alternative to the streets, gangs, the army..."

Kraven chuckled meaningfully and Moses grinned again.

"Sounded just like the army to me, so I told him to forget it. I'd forgotten you were there listening." Moses said to Fernando.

"Sounded good to me," Fernando picked up the conversation. "Very good and being the kid I was I didn't think there was any catch." He tugged on the cuff of the black shirt hanging outside his trousers. "At least not the catches I came to discover." He added morosely.

Kraven leaned forward then. "This painting is of the place where Fern and I along with Hill Tesano and a host of other misunderstood lads all met." He drowned what remained of his Scotch. "Oh there were catches, alright. All the things that the street life, gangs and the army provide all rolled into one."

"Jesus Fern..." Quest muttered.

"Right," Fernando smirked. "Took well over a year for me to wise up and get my ass the hell out of there. Getting in trouble at home and jail cells in King County was a helluva lot better than the shit we found on that island."

"So why would Persephone give this painting to Darby?" Carlos asked.

"I don't think that was her intention." Kraven answered. "Nile was off with T in Scotland. My guess is she planned on giving it to Nile in hopes of raising Muhammad's hackles."

"And now that he's dead?" Moses asked.

"Exactly- it makes no sense. I mean, what purpose does it all serve?" Yohan noted.

"Agreed. Only one thing's certain." Fernando didn't bother to continue.

"Should we be taking any precautions?" Quest said what his cousin wouldn't.

"I believe our women are fine." Kraven assured.

"I'm referring to our cousins." Quest clarified and slanted a glance toward Moses when Kraven's expression became less than assuring.

"Shit," Quay hissed and brought a fist down on the table. "Is this why they've got Tesanos sniffing around?"

"Only one sniffing around is Smoak." Quest corrected while silently thinking of Pike Tesano.

"I say we play it cool." Moses cast a stern look around the table. "No need to jump to any *overprotective measures*- not yet. Let's wait a bit, see what happens. Maybe we'll have a better shot at figuring out what the hell is going on a lot quicker."

Taurus puffed out his cheeks and reached for his drink. "Sure as hell can't hurt. We damn well don't have a thing else to go on."

Silently, the rest of the group agreed.

"Crickey," Kraven growled when he reached for his glass and realized it was empty. He was lifting his hand to request another when his vivid jades narrowed and his head tilted. "Good God," he breathed.

The phrase; and its delivery stifled conversation at the table. The guys focused on Kraven before turning to see what had roused such a reaction. In seconds, they'd each uttered similar phrases or simply grunted or cursed in outright appreciation.

Unlike her fiancés' bachelor send-off, Contessa Warren's party was the stuff X-rated bashes were made of. Following drinks, hors d'oeuvres and dirty movies in the special suite Sabra had reserved, the ladies took in a graphic all male revue in one of the many strip clubs right there at the resort. They'd all had a fantastic meal and decided it was time to drop in on the darkly intimidating *Sabra's Lair* for another drink. Afterwards, it was back to the suite for *more* drinks and dirty movies.

Spiked heels sank into the Lair's plush black carpeting as the ladies headed for the bar. Meanwhile, they turned the heads of virtually every male customer in the place.

"What the hell is she wearing?" Quest whispered almost to himself. Propping fist to chin he looked on in awe. His hazy stare was unwavering and focused on Michaela in a curve-clutching crimson jumpsuit. The bodice dipped almost to her bellybutton and offered a more than ample view of full bosom.

Quaysar and Moses were equally riveted. Their dark eyes narrowed in similar fashion toward their wives dressed almost identically in black suits with high collars. Tykira's gold choke-collar suit didn't dip as low as Mick's but was snug enough to leave nothing to the imagination. The cut out at the middle though, afforded a provocative view of her naval. Johari's tanned suit had a halter blouse styled bodice with its dip fashioned at the back and leaving her bare almost to the swell of her bottom.

Carlos reclined to a more relaxing position and focused on the dress gloving Dena's sultry frame. The creation was designed with one long sleeve. The entire left side of the frock was fashioned with cutaways that left patches of her flawless dark skin bare from neck to thigh.

Open-mouthed, Yohan studied the exotic Oriental number Melina slinked around in. The silk magenta qipao carried a daring split clear up the back and emphasized her spaghetti strapped heels.

Kraven tilted his head this way and that to take in every angle of Darby's slender busty frame gloved in an item that gave new meaning to the term 'little black dress'. The baby doll frock was actually dark turquoise with a halter neck. The bust ruching and empire waist cupped her chest and presented the honey brown mounds like they were the perfect gift. Matching turquoise heels were secured by the straps that spiraled about her legs.

Taurus held a hand to his brow and bit his lip on the need surging through him at the vision of the cream leather suit that looked as if it had been poured over Nile's svelte frame. The upsweep of her onyx tresses accentuated the short breast hugging blazer and diamond choker at her neck.

Fernando's translucent stare raked Contessa wearing a scrap of clothing that could hardly pass for a dress. The yellow daisy coloring of the garment brought increased richness to the already alluring tone of her honey skin. The *dress* itself appeared to be simply a mass of straps-some a tad thicker than others. Fernando celebrated the fact that the widest scraps of material covered (barely) her bosom and behind. He muttered a curse at every step she took for the action strained the material across every covered attribute that was inches from being revealed.

"Where the fuck is she going in that?" He hissed.

Moses shook his head and continued to ravage Johari by the sheer intensity of his stare. "I'm guessing they've already been." He told his brother.

"And look at this shit." Quay muttered, watching as several men left their tables to approach the eight beauties at the bar.

Whatever conversations on tap for the evening's agenda were completely forgotten as all attention focused on the Lair's new arrivals.

It didn't take long for the eight ladies to dash the hopes of the gentlemen whose propositions ranged from the sweet and suave to the seductive and downright X-rated. The defeated men took it all in stride as though deep down they knew they didn't stand a chance. Unfortunately, the speediness of their departures in no way quelled the agitation of the only men in the Lair who'd decided *not* to approach the bar.

The girls enjoyed their drinks and a bit more conversation before making their exit. Once they were gone, the Ramsey/ DeBurgh/McPhereson party decided another round of hard liquor was definitely needed.

***

Following a virtual battle with Sabra; in which she emerged the victor, the guys found someone to bribe for info on the location of the Warren bachelorette party. For an extra $50 bucks, they scored a room key to the split level suite on the other end of the executive offices.

It was easy to guess at some of what was going on inside. The music pounded and caused the heavy pine door to vibrate a little. When Fernando inserted the key and pushed open the door, his companion's mouths fell open at the visions before their eyes.

Fernando spotted Contessa at the wall which housed an impressive sound system. With drinks in hand, she, Nile and Dena danced energetically to the Mary Jane Girls' "*Candy Man*". The song filled the room with its affective beat and lyrics. Though the music effectively drowned their voices, it didn't stop the threesome from singing their hearts out. Taurus and Carlos shifted their stances to obtain a better look at their wives and loved everything they saw.

Michaela and Melina occupied the sofa and coffee table respectively. Both stood on their chosen furnishings and gyrated to the beat of the song as they too sang with all the gumption they could muster.

Quest folded his arms over the navy shirt hanging outside his jeans and smiled. He didn't think he'd ever tire of just happening upon one of his wife's dance sessions.

Yohan; on the other hand, rarely caught his wife offering such a show. Like the rest of his cohorts, he stood open mouthed and staring.

Along the staircase, Tykira's, Johari's and Darby's faces were hidden amidst a wealth of tresses flying about them in a sandy red, onyx and honey blonde blur.

Moses, Quay and Kraven simply relaxed against a wall and took in the enticing show which heated up when the Mary Jane Girls' tune faded into the sultry reggae groove of Mad Cobra's "*Flex*". Appreciative smiles curved their mouths in unison and the guys were on another level of heaven.

That is, until Quay felt a punch in his bicep. Turning, he found his cousin fuming in the doorway. Sabra's immediate ranting was greatly muted by the music but that didn't stop her from strolling in and giving them all a piece of her mind.

Of course none of the guys looked too kindly upon having their entertainment interrupted. The Mad Cobra tune was fading into Hall and Oates' *"I Can't Go For That"* when they all slanted Quay a knowing look.

Quaysar began walking forward as the smooth grooves of the song started to vibrate the door again. Sabra didn't realize she'd been backed out into the corridor until Quay leaned close to kiss her cheek.

"Good Night," he said.

"Dammit Quay I wanna know what the hell y'all are gonna do?"

Quay's grin sparked his striking right dimple. "Ah, ah, ah Sabra. What happens in Vegas..." he sang and shut the door in his cousin's frowning face.

FIVE

Thursday~ Chicago...

Mid morning found the bride and groom in slight debate over the guys invasion of the bachelorette party the night before.

"I mean, at least me and my girls were decent enough not to barge in on *your* party."

"Mmm hmm," Fernando grunted while securing the clasp on his watch. "What do you call that stunt in the bar?"

Contessa didn't fake confusion. "We had no idea y'all were there."

"Come off it."

County walked on ahead of him down the stairway. "My fiancés' a jerk," she sang.

Fernando caught the edge of her white T-shirt before she took the last step. County refused to acknowledge the bumps of anticipation riddling her skin when he trapped her against the banister and trailed his nose along her jaw.

"Are any of you really that upset over what went on in that suite once the lights went out?"

She rolled her eyes and tried to angle her face away from his touch. A meaningful tingle stirred someplace at the mention of the completely scandalous events that occurred on each level and over every square foot of the elaborate suite. Contessa knew it'd be a long time before she stopped blushing over memories of Prince's sexy crooning and the moans filling the darkened suite with sounds of desire.

The bell rang and County flashed Fernando a scathing look as she headed to answer the door.

"That's what I thought," he murmured, a smile curving his mouth as he leaned on the banister.

County pulled open the front door and found herself staring into her mirror image. Neena Warren stood on the other side and uttered an excited shriek in unison with her daughter. They fell into hugs and laughter seconds later.

"Hey Ms. Neena," Fernando was saying when he leaned in for his hug and kiss.

"Baby," Neena relished the embrace then bit her lip like a school girl as she watched her soon-to-be son-in-law make his exit. "Have I told you how incredible he is?" Neena whispered.

County shrugged. "'Bout a million times. But I swear he can be aggravating as hell sometimes."

Neena fell in step with her daughter as they strolled the foyer. "Well that can't be too hard to accept once you get down to the uh…meat of the matter."

Sending her mother a sly look, County nudged her shoulder. "You're a dirty lady, Neena Warren."

Neena shrugged. "Getting older's gotta have *some* perks."

"Seriously Bunny," Neena said once their laughter mellowed. "I apologize for being a day early."

"I had a feeling you would be after our talk."

"Actually it was the call from your Aunt Corinth that did it."

County muttered a curse. "They had it comin'." She said in reference to Corinth's daughters Monique and Trenique.

"Baby was it really necessary in front of Mick and the rest of your soon to be family?"

"Yes it was." County hung her mother's coat and slammed the closet door. "I hope the bitches told everybody else in their sorry family!"

"Contessa!"

"I don't want 'em here, Mama!"

Neena fidgeted with the diamond pin adorning her gray silk blouse. "Not even your father, baby? Not even on your wedding day?"

"Especially not him and especially not on my wedding day." County studied the chic press and curl style that flattered her mother's lovely face, and then she frowned. "How could you push for this after what he did? I just can't understand that, Mama."

"Oh Baby," Neena drew her daughter close and kissed her cheek. "Have you told Fernando?"

"No," County pulled away and rubbed her arms to ward off a sudden chill. "He never needs to know that."

"He could easily find out, you know?" Neena trailed her fingers through County's short, dark crop. "I'm surprised Monique and Tren didn't say it just to hurt you when they were here."

"Well they aren't gonna have another chance. Security will be tight and they'll know that nobody with the last name Samuels gets past the front gate."

Neena shook her head and watched her hot-tempered daughter stomp on ahead.

***

The remainder of the day brought the arrival of the Ramsey elders. Though several wouldn't show up at Mick's house until the day of the wedding; a few dropped in for hellos and to bestow best wishes on the happy couple.

"You two look very at ease to say you've had two boys and a baby girl to take care of for the better part of a week." Mick was saying as she hugged her in-laws.

Damon squeezed her closer before pressing a kiss to her temple and pulling back to flash his striking double dimpled grin.

"Those three are a piece of cake compared to their dads." He spoke in reference to Quest and Quay.

Catrina nudged Mick's shoulder and winked. "At least we can give back those three once the fun is over."

Nile arrived with Quincee while Michaela, Damon and Catrina were still laughing.

"She's a doll." Nile marveled and kissed Damon and Catrina.

Someone called the elder Ramseys who excused themselves. It didn't take long for Mick's sharp perceptive skills to notice the apprehension filling her sister's gaze.

"Tell me," Mick urged.

Nile bounced Quincee and smiled when the child laughed. "I was just wondering if you'd ever consider visiting our family—*your* family in California?"

The apprehension took residence in Michaela's amber stare then. Sighing, she stepped close and began to fidget with the pink frills on Quincee's dress. "I prayed for such a day and now that it's here…I'm scared as hell." She winced and looked up at Nile. "Does that make sense?"

"Perfect sense," Nile laughed when Quincee tugged at the collar of her polo top. "But there's something else you should keep in mind. I'll be with you all the way."

Mick laughed as though it were a fact she should never have forgotten. With Quincee between them, they shared a hug.

Damon and Catrina sought a moment of refuge on a remote sofa in the sitting room.

"What's up?" Damon murmured, kissing his wife's forehead when she rested her face in the crook of her neck.

"Just never thought we'd live to see Quest *and* Quay both fathers, both in happy marriages with women they adore…"

"Yeah," Damon snuggled down a bit on the sofa and drew his wife closer, "it was *touch and go* there for a while, wasn't it?"

The couple shared a hearty chuckle over Damon's suggestive yet accurate choice of words.

"And the rest of the boys," Catrina mused curling her trouser-clad legs beneath her. "It's just really wonderful how everything turned out despite the forces trying to ruin it all."

"And no one's heard a peep out of Marc," Damon sighed. "What do you think about that?"

"I try not to think about that."

Catrina propped her chin on his shoulder. "And everyone else?"

"Carmen and Georgia could care less- same goes for West. I don't think any of 'em care one way or another what's happening to the man."

Catrina curled closer to her husband. "Your brother's a sleeping dog best left lying."

Damon closed his eyes. "And I hope he stays that way."

***

Dinner was a hearty conversation rich affair. The Ramsey elders who'd arrived that day, stayed on hand for the catered feast. Neena Warren was embraced by the older set like they'd all been friends for ages.

Contessa was thrilled by the progression of events since none of her father's family showed their faces at the dinner. Laughter and boisterous toasts were the order of the evening of course. Westin Ramsey however brought the night's festivities back to order with his special toast to the bride and groom.

As the eldest Ramsey son, West spoke to Fernando in the manner of a father. He relayed words of pride to the younger man as well as words of admiration for the type of man Fernando had become in the face of many obstacles.

"Hold fast and communicate with your husband Contessa." Westin said. "You'll never go wrong if you stay true to those things. Fern, treasure your wife and draw strength from your union. View her as your equal in all things and your bond will span decades."

Fernando and Contessa linked hands from their place at the long table.

"To the bride and groom!" Westin bellowed.

Glasses raised and caught the twinkle of the candlelight glowing in the room.

"To the bride and groom!" Everyone cheered.

***

Following the feast of roasted chicken quarters, wild rice, broccoli and mushroom sauté, corn muffins with honey butter and key lime pie, the group adjourned to the living room for coffee and drinks.

Briselle Ramsey caught her sister-in-law's eye across the room and pointed.

"Let's go while Georgia's occupied." Bri said to Carmen and joined in when the woman laughed.

"You're looking happier than I've ever seen you. Care to share?" Briselle asked while they walked toward the den.

"Life is good." Carmen Ramsey almost purred with a sun-bright smile.

"And Marc's missing." Briselle noted with a saucy tilt of her head.

Carmen hugged her petite frame. "That makes it even better. I hope he's rotting."

"Carmen," Briselle waited until they were behind the closed doors of the den. "Did you have anything to do with that?"

"Why Bri how in the world would I know about doing something like that? Why in the world would I care?" She added while pulling invisible lint from her fitted lavender suit coat.

"It's all we've talked about lately, remember?" Briselle's sparkling stare was sharp. "At first I thought it was all a tease-outrageous fantasizing…" she stepped closer and clutched Carmen's arm. "Now I'm getting the feeling that somewhere along the line it became real for you."

Carmen suddenly turned the tables and gripped Briselle's arm. "It was always real for me." Her stony expression vanished as quickly as it had emerged. She kissed Briselle's cheek and left the den.

***

County had been looking for her mother and was told by Crane and Josephine that Neena had been called out to the foyer.

County went to investigate, turning livid and more than a little nervous at the sight of the woman talking and laughing with Lincoln Samuels.

"What the hell's he doin' here?" County's eyes threw daggers toward her father.

"Contess-"

"Hey Babylove," Lincoln interrupted his ex-wife and approached his daughter.

County bristled and rolled her eyes. "Mama when you're done here, I need you in the living room."

"Alright County that's it!" Neena snapped. "I've had about all I can stand of this nastiness!"

"Oh Mama that can't be. I don't think you've had nearly enough not when you're being stupid enough to stand here and listen to this fool's excuses!"

"Alright Conty, no more!" Lincoln blared, his handsome round face tight with tension. "You may hate me, but I won't stand quiet and watch you be cruel to your mama!"

"Oh please!" County was beyond caring. "Cruel? Did you say cruel?" She propped fists to her hips and glared. "Cruel…what the hell could be more cruel that leaving your wife for another man?!"

Silence came down across the foyer like an anvil. As if she were snapping from a trance, County covered her mouth behind both hands stunned that she'd finally spoken the words she'd longed to say to her father. Then, her lashes fluttered and she realized she wasn't alone with her parents. A crowd had filled the space.

"God," she croaked and raced up the stairs.

SJX

Friday...

The bedroom door locked behind Contessa following her outburst the night before. The guys had to practically sit on Fernando to keep him from kicking down the door to get to County. She would only whisper through the door to Michaela that she couldn't face anyone that night and would be okay by morning.

Mick was knocking by eight a.m. on Friday. She gave the thumbs up sign to everyone hovering on the second floor landing, when the locks clicked.

"What's up?" Mick looked around the room for any sign of broken vases or other fragile items.

County barely grunted a greeting and trudged back to the rumpled bed where she'd tossed frantically the night before.

Mick lay next to her against the pillow-lined headboard and trailed her fingers through County's unkempt hair.

"They gone?" County's voice was half muffled in a pillow.

Mick smiled. "Josephine and Crane asked Ms. Neena to stay with them-there's an extra room out in the guest house. Your dad left right after you...went upstairs."

County groaned suddenly and clutched hair between her fingers. "Will that man *ever* stop humiliating me?"

"Honey, shh..."

"No Mick," County pushed her best friend away. "My aunts couldn't wait to spread the word about their gay brother-guess they wanted to beat everybody else to it. The whole neighborhood knew by the time me and Mama were forced to go live out there."

"Honey..." Mick kissed the back of County's head.

"My life was hell," she spoke on a sob. "One day I said 'fuck it'. I wasn't gonna give 'em the satisfaction of seein' me cry another day."

"And did holding everything in help?"

County laughed shortly in response to Mick's question. "No- hence last night's outburst." She pushed herself up a bit on the bed. "Mama always made me be respectful. In spite of the shit Daddy pulled, she'd never let me tell that jackass what I thought of him. What happened last night would've happened whenever I saw the man." She shrugged and bit on her thumbnail. "Guess it was better last night than at the wedding, huh?"

Mick nudged County's thigh with her knee. "So you feelin' any better now?"

"I don't know," she wiped the hem of her shirt across her nose. "I don't know how I feel except embarrassed beyond belief that I spilled my family beans in front of everyone."

Mick cupped her chin. "That's family- they understand."

County sniffled again. "I never wanted them to know-especially Fernando."

"He's about out of his mind, you know?" Mick leaned back on the headboard and massaged her nose. "Yohan couldn't even hold him down. Finally the guys had to get him drunk enough to pass out."

County looked sympathetic for a moment and then dashed away the emotion. "I can't see him."

"Why?"

"Hell Mick, I don't want his pity." She folded her arms across her chest. "I'd rather hear the jokes and name-calling I suffered through as a kid."

"No you wouldn't." Mick sat on her knees in the middle of the bed. "Expecting cruelty is way easier than enduring it and you know that's your mask talkin."

"You're right." County's uneasy look returned and she knocked a fist against the denim Capris Mick wore. "I don't know how to face him- so ashamed…"

"Honey why? You're not the one in love with men- oops." She winced playfully. "Got my sexes mixed up there, didn't I?" She winked upon drawing a smile from County.

"Anyway you've got to do something. The man's out there with the hangover from hell and pacing like crazy." Mick wrung her hands. "I don't need him kicking down the door. I'm tryin' to sell this place, you know?"

Contessa's smile remained but she still looked uneasy.

"Look on the bright side," Mick smoothed a few wayward locks behind County's ear. "Unlike me, at least *you* know who your father is."

Laughter filled the room then. It was loud, long, refreshing and welcomed.

"Thanks girl," County pulled Mick into a tight hug.

"Okay?" Mick asked when they drew apart.

Contessa closed her eyes while nodding.

In spite of his pacing and rampaging, Fernando was subdued when the door finally opened and Michaela waved him inside.

County stood from the bed and held the gaze with her fiancé until the door closed and they were alone.

"Ramsey I-"

Fernando simply waved her quiet and bounded over to pull her into his strong embrace. Contentment swelled through County, curving her mouth into a smile as she held onto the man she loved.

***

By mid-morning, the upsets of the previous evening were practically forgotten. The wedding breakfast was turned into a wedding brunch that went off without a hitch.

"Stop being so stupid," Fernando ordered his fiancée while they enjoyed quiet time on the porch where he massaged her feet.

"I just didn't think you'd want to marry me if you ever found out." She wiggled her toes inside navy tights. "You have no idea how much crap I heard coming up. Somewhere somebody told me it was an inherited thing. Our kids could be-"

Fernando sat up suddenly and brought his index finger within inches of her nose. "Shut it, do you hear me Contessa?" He waited for her nod. "You are not an ignorant woman and that's exactly what you're sounding like." He rolled his eyes and leaned back on the wood bench they shared. "Whatever our kids are or aren't won't change the fact that we'll love them, will it?"

"No. Never."

"Alright then. So shut up already."

County smiled. "Ramsey?"

"What?"

"Do you realize we're talking about kids- *our* kids?"

"Yeah, so let me enjoy that instead of all this other nonsense you're talkin'."

County crept closer then to snuggle against his big frame. "I love you Ramsey."

"I love you too. Now shut up."

***

"Girl please, it's not a problem. Unpredictability is a given with a job like yours." Mick was saying as she spoke with Sybilla Ramsey by phone. "And anyway, you can do no wrong by the bride after giving her the gift of the week at that hedonist's ranch in Maui."

Sybilla laughed. "Yeah, I thought that'd go over well, but don't any of you dare tell Sabra. The wench would kill me if she knew I was patronizing any resort besides hers."

"My lips are sealed." Mick laughed. "Listen Bill, thanks for calling and letting us know what was up. Did you still want to talk to Moses?" Michaela heard Bill saying yes as she caught Moses' eye while he made his way past her study.

"It's Bill," she handed him the phone and gave him privacy.

The easy tone Sybilla had used with Mick faded and was replaced by a far more strained tinge when her cousin's deep voice filled the line.

"It's a new assignment Mo," she explained when he questioned her absence.

"Are congrats in order?" he asked.

"Not even. They gave me a file with Caiphus Tesano's picture inside Moses."

"You don't say?" He leaned against the desk.

"I *do* say and why don't *you* sound surprised?"

"I am."

"Bullshit. What do you know?"

Moses cupped a hand beneath his arm and turned serious. "I swear I don't know anything yet. But with everything I'm learning this isn't all that much of a surprise."

"Hell Moses, I could be working with him. *With* him- not against him to put him behind bars. Are you hinting that we may be on the same side?"

"Pieces are still being put in place B, but that's exactly what I'm telling you. Just play your cards close to the vest, alright?" He looked round to see if anyone was making their way into the study. "How much do your bosses know?" He asked her then.

"They know there's no love lost between me and him."

Moses grinned. "You may have to get over that, you know?"

"When you give me more to go on, I'll consider it."

"Fair enough."

"Stay in touch Moses."

"I promise. Love you. Be safe."

"Always."

Her connection broke then.

***

The phone in Michaela's old study proved to be the busiest machine in the house that day. Sabra called shortly after lunch hoping to speak with Quay or Ty. Instead, Sabra's mother Georgia Ramsey, overheard Mick greeting her daughter and just had to be the first to speak. Some fifteen minutes later, Sabra was connected to Tykira.

"Just calm down alright?" Ty snapped her fingers toward Quay and covered the mouthpiece when he was near. "She's hysterical."

Quay took the receiver and put the call on speaker. "What's goin' on Sabe? Calm-calm down and talk to us."

A heavy breath came through the speaker. "I've just been told that the penthouse of my second tower has been reserved by Smoak Tesano."

Quaysar cursed and Sabra resumed her hysterics.

"Can he do that?" Ty asked while Sabra ranted. "She stays so busy can he just occupy it that easily?"

"Smoak's co-owner of the place," Quay explained over Sabra's shuddering.

"Fuck that!"

Quay and Ty looked down at the speaker when Sabra's verbal skills suddenly returned.

"That bastard was co-owner up until the time I got away from his hateful ass! He's got no interest in my new architecture."

Quay waved off the explanation. "He still owns enough of a chunk to easily take occupation of an entire floor."

"What am I gonna do?" Sabra moaned.

"When's he coming?" Quay winced when his cousin sucked her teeth over the line.

"His *people* didn't say when- meaning the floor has to remain unoccupied. Shit! This mess is gonna cost me hand over fist."

Quay didn't bother asking his cousin to calm down then since he was just as on edge about the situation.

"Look just tell me when he gets there, alright?" Quay took the phone off speaker and pressed the receiver into his chest. "Try and get her calm before she hangs up, okay?" He kissed Tykira's cheek and left the room.

***

Sabella Ramsey snapped her fingers, remembering the wrap she was about to leave behind. She was on her way out of the hotel suite she was sharing with her mother while in Chicago for the wedding.

Belle grabbed the lavender diamond print wrap and was on her way out when distinctive chimes caught her ears. She recognized her mother's cell phone ring tone and frowned. Carmen Ramsey never ventured too far from the device. Belle set aside the wrap and tried to pinpoint the location of the sound.

"Bet she's going crazy without it." She sighed, following the tone to the overnight bag on an armchair.

Belle only glanced at the faceplate once she'd fished the phone out from the bottom of the bag. Another frowned marred her brow just as the cell's backlight clicked off. She took a second look and her mouth fell open.

***

County braced herself to turn and walk the minute she saw her parents across the restaurant dining room.

"Ah, ah, ah…" Fernando's hand tightened on her arm.

"I haven't spoken to the man at length for years." She raised her chin. "Last time we had a meal together I hadn't even hit puberty."

"Well now's the time for new things, right?" Fernando reasoned, rubbing his thumb across the satin sleeve of County's dress. "Maybe this could be one of those new things."

She bowed her head then. "Ramsey…"

"Hey, hey…" he leaned close to nudge his nose along her nape. "I'm right here and I'm not goin' anywhere. I'm right here." For emphasis, he pulled her back next to him.

The contact gave her the strength to move forward, not stopping until Neena and Lincoln noticed her approaching.

"Hey Ms. Neena," Fernando greeted the woman with a hug and kiss when she stood. "Have you guys ordered?" He asked while shaking hands with Linc Samuels.

"Just drinks." Neena said as they all took their seats. "Is this a new place Fernando? I thought I knew all the restaurants on this end of town."

Fernando looked around the establishment. "Yes ma'am, a manager at my club told me about it a few months ago, but this is the first time I had to check it out. Thought it'd be good to try something new," he slanted a meaningful look toward his fiancée.

"Well I think it's a beautiful place."

"My baby's the beauty." Linc interrupted his ex-wife to compliment his daughter.

County could barely nod. "Thank you," she managed, catching her mother's and Fernando's stern looks.

"So how did you two meet?" Linc asked, once the waiter left with their orders.

"Contessa's publishing house was doing a book on my family. Official release is in a few months, right babe?" Fernando nodded when County smiled.

Lincoln's handsome face glowed as he nodded over Fernando's explanation. "Contessa House, I talk about it all the time. Actually I should say I brag about it all the time."

"Brag?" County blurted.

"Almost everyday." Linc tugged at the cuff of his brown tweed suit coat. "My clients are probably sick of it, but they're too decent to argue with their account manager."

"You talk about me to your business associates?"

"I'm proud of you Conty- all your accomplishments." He spread his hands. "I take no credit for how lovely you are- how lovely your life is- all the great things you've done. I can only be thankful for the relief and joy I feel. Knowing how well you turned out in spite of all you went through because of me…" His head bowed and he appeared to need a moment to compose himself.

"I'm sorry Conty, so sorry…my selfishness and stupidity kept me from saying this when you were younger. Then later, it was pure disgust over the way I handled things with you and your mother." Linc squeezed Neena's hand. "I told your mother you had every right to not want to speak to me. I knew I'd wait until you could- after all I did, it was the very least I could do."

"I'm sorry Conty," his brown eyes were moist with tears, "if there's any way- no matter how small- that you could fit me into your life, I'd take it. I'd take it and treasure it like I never treasured anything else in my life."

Through blurry eyes, County watched her father extend his hand toward her. The tears hit her cheeks when she reached out to let her fingers rest against his palm.

SEVEN

Saturday...

The wedding day arrived bright, sunny and full of promise. Mostly everyone had the same thoughts of how very long the last several days had seemed. Still, the outcomes and new beginnings on the horizon gave everyone the hope that it would all be worth it.

"You look like a princess." Mick said when she walked up behind Contessa seated on the vanity chair.

County smiled, drawing strength from her friend's embrace. "I do look pretty good, don't I?" She winked. The teasing light in her eyes however took on a more serene appeal as she observed herself in the gown. The creation fit like a glove. If there were a more apt description, then Contessa couldn't think of it. At her calves, the dress flared out like a bell while a train of shimmering satin flowed behind. Lace sleeves covered her arms and half her hands. They were under set by delicate chiffon as was the scooping bodice that accentuated the fullness of her bosom.

"Sabella's a genius," Michaela sighed in pure awe of the gown her husband's cousin had designed as a gift to the bride and groom.

"I agree." County nodded, loving the way her gleaming silver choker offset the creation. "The woman should have her own line. Creating such things for people just to wear on a stage seems like such a waste."

"Ah, I don't know." Mick smoothed her hands over County's arms. "I think she's pretty happy with all those awards she collects each year." She said in reference to Sabella's acclaimed work as a theatrical costume designer. "You ready for this?" She asked then and gave her best friend a tight squeeze.

County's lashes fluttered. "I never thought *this* would come. Told myself I didn't need or want *this*."

"And now?"

Laughing then, a wealth of tears caused her brown eyes to glisten. "Now I can't imagine how I survived without *this*." She swallowed and blinked hard. "Michaela thank you- for sticking by me through all the craziness."

"It was all worth it, don't you think?"

Satin rustled as County turned on the seat. "So worth it," she whispered and hugged Mick tight.

A quick knock fell upon the bedroom door some moments later.

"Alright?" Mick prompted, nodding until Contessa did the same.

Dapper in white tuxedos, Moses and Yohan waited in the hallway. The two of them were giving away the bride. After gazing in awe at County, the guys exchanged looks.

"Is our crazy brother really deserving of all that beauty?" Yohan asked Moses who only shook his head and studied the breathtaking gown and Contessa in it.

County laughed and waved her hand. "Thanks guys."

The brothers leaned forward in unison and kissed her cheek.

"No thanks necessary for telling the truth." Moses said.

The guys each offered an arm which County accepted.

"Let's go get you married." Yohan said.

The foursome left the bedroom with Michaela collecting the bride's bouquet and the flowing train of the gown.

***

The day was perfect for an outdoor wedding. A newly constructed gazebo would house the wedding party while the bride and groom exchanged their vows. Guests in attendance finished up last minute drinks and were locating their seats once the announcement was made that the ceremony was about to begin.

Georgia Ramsey placed her emptied champagne flute to the tray of a passing waiter while another guest did the same. The smile on her face froze when she made eye contact with her ex-husband Felix Cade.

Blinking owlishly, Georgia could do little more than take in the still incredible dark features of the man she'd once worshipped.

"Beautiful as ever G," Felix complimented as he stepped forward to trail the back of his hand across her cheek.

"What are you doing here?" Her voice was hardly a whisper.

Felix shrugged beneath the tailored tuxedo jacket. "Couldn't ignore an invite from my nephew."

"Why are you here Felix?" Her voice held a little more strength, but not much.

Felix gave a one-shoulder shrug and didn't bother to mask the appreciation in his dark eyes as they surveyed her oval face now sharply beautiful with the onset of age. He shook off the spell he'd surrendered to. "Hoped to see you," he said.

"That's rich," Georgia's laughter possessed an unconscious lightness. "No one goes *anywhere* hoping to see me."

Felix stepped closer and kissed her cheek. "That's 'cause they don't know you G." He said and walked on.

"How long will you keep this from me, Mama?"

Carmen Ramsey smiled and waved at someone across the aisle. "Baby what is it you want me to say? I don't even know what you're talking about."

Sabella balled a gloved fist. "I'm talking about what I tried talking to you about last night and then again earlier today." Her wide stare grew wider still as she watched a calm envelope her mother. The affect was almost tangible and it set Belle more on edge than she wanted to acknowledge. "Mama what's going on?"

"Baby nothing," Carmen laughed.

"Knowing a man like Brogue is never nothing."

"Oh you," Carmen smoothed a hand across the double split lavender skirt Belle wore. "Now that's Isak talking."

Sabella bristled suddenly as though hearing her ex-husband's name had tapped against something inside her. She cleared her throat, averting her gaze before her mother noticed.

It was too late, but Carmen said nothing. She was satisfied that her daughter's mind was too consumed by images of Isak Tesano to question her further about his cousin.

The distinctive chords of *"Here Comes The Bride"* began only to merge into an exquisite rendering of DeBarge's *"All This Love."*

Everyone stood.

Contessa held onto Moses' and Yohan's arms for both support and courage but her brown eyes were locked on Fernando's translucent ones as he stood there with the reverend at the end of the aisle.

In his expression, County found all the support, courage and strength she knew she'd ever need.

Michaela completed her march as Matron of Honor. She turned to take her place and gave her best friend a happy smile of encouragement. Moses and Yohan each kissed County's hand before applying the same treat to her cheek. Then, they assumed their second roles as the groom's best men. They clapped Fernando's shoulder, hugged him and turned him toward his fiancée.

Everyone took their seats and the ceremony began. The Reverend Gregor Sims' words were passionate and persuasive. The vows spoken between the bride and groom; however, were what brought tears to several pairs of eyes.

"Contessa," Fernando began and cleared his throat on the swell of emotion that had found its way there. "I adore you." His gaze crinkled when it met hers. "I desire you, I love you and I vow to treasure you- each day as my equal, my partner, my lover and my very best friend. I vow to never let you forget that I'm here to add strength to your strength, passion to your passion...temper to your temper."

The last drew soft chuckling from the audience.

Fernando cleared his throat again. "I'm yours. Forever. *Forever.* I love you."

County blinked several times to dash away the tears blurring her vision.

"Ramsey," she smiled shyly. "Fernando. I love you. In that love I find no need for masks, no need for fear, no need for uncertainty. I trust in your love and in your strength. I vow to love you through whatever challenges may await us. I vow to love you through every disagreement." She laughed when he winked. "I vow to love you through every triumph. I'm yours forever and forever I love you."

"Amen," Reverend Sims said once the rings were exchanged. "By the power vested in me by the State of Illinois, I now pronounce you husband and wife."

A wave of cheers, laughter and applause practically drowned out the reverend's instruction to Fernando to kiss his bride.

Following the toasts, first dance and cutting of the cake, it was time for the removal of the groom's cummerbund and the bride's garter.

County performed her duty demurely and was seated with her heart pounding as her husband eased down the garter with a seductive slowness.

"Hurry up, will you?" She hissed while trying to maintain her sweet smile.

Fernando's grin was purely wicked. "You know I want to be removing more than this damn garter."

"This is a family event," she reminded him even as a tiny needy sound curled in the back of her throat when his fingers ventured beyond the garter. "What would your Aunt Georgia say?"

Laughing then, Fernando finished with the garter and stood to toss the garment round his index finger. He whirled it toward the crowd of cheering men and then turned to swing County up against his chest.

"Let's find out." He said.

***

Quay took a glass of champagne from a passing waiter while he and Tykira danced. He tilted the glass toward Ty to offer her a swallow and then drank deeply when she shook her head.

Instead, Ty cuddled closer to her husband. She wedged her face into the crook of his neck, bared by the open shirt collar when he'd undone his bowtie.

"We won't be here long if you keep that up." Quay warned.

"Sorry, I just feel so good." She breathed in his scent as a contented smile curved her mouth. "Guess it's just the happiness of the day."

Quay locked his arms about her waist and let the champagne flute dangle at the small of her back. "You do look more calmed down," he noted when he leaned back to observe her lovely molasses-dark face. "Did you finish all your projects?"

"They were really weighing on me." She nodded.

"I could tell." He pushed at the long spiral curl dangling from her chignon. "I didn't like it. I don't want you working so hard if it's gonna wear you down that way."

"You're sweet." She kissed his cheek and then brushed the back of her hand across the flawless surface. "But work isn't totally to blame. I just wanted to settle those projects while I could. My doctor said I probably won't feel like lifting my head off the pillow in the next few weeks."

Quay took another swallow of champagne before her words caused him to frown. "Your doctor?"

"We took so long to find the right time, the right time found us." She shrugged.

Quay lightly necklaced his free hand around the base of her throat. "What are you trying to tell me?"

"You're gonna be a dad again." Ty bit her lip and waited on his reaction.

He leaned forward then as though he'd lost strength to stand.

Ty smiled but pretended not to notice. "You're gonna have to wait a little longer for this one to come than the twins."

Dazedly, Quay set a hand to her tummy and then looked up suddenly before leaning in to ply her with the deepest kiss.

Quest and Mick were laughing like two kids while watching Quincee pull herself up to stand next to the sectional sofa that filled a corner of the den.

Quincee's curls bobbed over her head and her dimpled smile emerged as if she knew she'd done something incredible. Gray eyes wide, she began to move on tentative steps; making her way round the angle of the sofa, toward her parents.

"Incredible," Quest sighed. He pulled his little girl into his arms when she crawled the last few inches separating them. "Do you know how incredible you are?" He whispered and kissed her tiny nose.

Laughing gleefully, Quincee held her dad's face; as best she could between her tiny palms, and planted a more suitable kiss to his mouth.

Mick's eyes sparkled with happy tears as she took in the scene before leaning over to kiss the back of her baby's head. Sitting back, she studied the room they shared.

"House will be listed next week." She said.

"Having second thoughts?" He asked and reached over to pull her close to him and Quincee.

"No," Mick shook her head against his shoulder. "No I'm good with it. I know Driggers would be happy, because I'm happy." She raked fingers through Quinn's curls. "So very happy," she looked up at Quest then and they shared a kiss before breaking away to tickle and hug their child.

Taurus, Kraven, Carlos, Moses and Yohan were enjoying drinks and idle conversation while lounging on the sun drenched patio that overlooked the area where the wedding had taken place. They'd been out there little over half an hour when their wives joined them. For a time, the group enjoyed the ease of the afternoon.

"What are our chances of staying this way?" Dena winced when she heard the words leaving her tongue. "Sorry," she whispered as Carlos settled her more snug against him.

"No need, love," Kraven's grin was melancholy as he toyed with Darby's hair. "I've been wondering the same."

Taurus grimaced while fiddling with the chiffon hem of Nile's dress. "Whatever affects the Tesanos is gonna affect us in some way as long as Belle, Sabra and Bill are part of the picture."

"Do you think they need protection?" Johari asked from her curled position against Moses.

"Guys I think we're all getting ahead of ourselves here." Melina was saying as Yohan pulled her off the arm of the chair and into his lap.

"I agree." Nile traced Taurus' hand where it lay on her knee. "From what I understand things have pretty much fizzled with those relationships." She shrugged uncertainly. "Maybe they'll remain that way."

"Maybe," Darby breathed, resting her head back on Kraven's shoulder while sandwiching one of his hands between both of hers. "Still…folks often get drawn into things they've got no clue about or expect."

"And I think we're worrying over a bunch of nothin' right now." Moses spoke up. "One thing about our three cousins is that they've learned the hard way how to take care of themselves."

"Damn right." Yohan's baritone rumbled. "Heaven help any Tesano who don't think twice about steppin' into the ring with them."

The notion brought smiles to everyone's faces. Moments later, they all raised their glasses in silent toasts.

***

"Stop!" County hissed and popped Fernando's roaming hands. "Everyone's gonna know what we've been up to."

"Well hell yeah, if Aunt Georgie's still around." Fernando turned County to face him when she laughed. "Are you ready?"

"Very." Her voice reflected her happiness.

Fernando tilted up her chin and began to nuzzle the curve of her jaw. "Think you can handle having me for a husband? I'm a pretty demanding guy, you know?"

"I can handle you." County linked her arms about his neck.

Fernando drew her into a crushing embrace. "I love you." He sighed.

"I love you." She sighed back.

"Let's get out of here," he growled against her mouth.

Contessa conducted her final bridal duty of the day. Calling all single ladies young and young at heart to the floor, she prepared to toss the bouquet. Cheers and mounds of surprised laughter filled the air when Carmen caught the arrangement of scented flowers.

"Too much!" County cried when she and Fernando raced down the porch steps amidst flurries of pink, yellow and white confetti towards a gleaming white motorcycle that waited.

"You're a crazy man!" She told her husband when he lifted her onto the back of the vehicle.

She set her chin to his shoulder once he'd settled in before her. "Another trip to the desert, Ramsey?"

Fernando turned and kissed his wife's cheek. "If you like," he murmured into her skin.

County banded her arms about his waist and squeezed. "As long as we're together."

He took her hand and planted a hard kiss to her palm. "Always love, always."

The motorcycle roared to life and Mr. and Mrs. Fernando and Contessa Ramsey zoomed off amidst roars of laughter and best wishes.

Hi Everyone,

Hope you all had a great time at the wedding. For those of you who figured all those trips to Vegas would result in new Ramseys, guess you were right. Perhaps the newlyweds Fernando and Contessa will be next with a precious bundle. Only time will tell…

At any rate, I hope you soaked in all the happiness. From here, things return to serious and downright unsettling.

Prepare yourselves for the origin of all the drama. *Book of Scandal: The Ramsey Elders* is next.

As always, please email me your thoughts and comments. altonya@lovealtonya.com

Love and Blessings,
Al
www.lovealtonya.com

AND NOW…...

A preview of the upcoming release "Book of Scandal- The Ramsey Elders"….

~CHAPTER ONE~

Savannah, Georgia~ Summer 1960…

Thirteen year old Carmen Ramsey gave a frustrated tug at the hem of the flowing chiffon skirt of her dress. Jackie Wilson's *"Doggin Around"* had fast become one of her favorites when it was released earlier that summer, but even the song's affective rhythms weren't inducing a positive effect on her mood. If the annual Ramsey cotillion wasn't over soon she truly believed she'd scream.

While her sister Georgia thrived on such festivities, Carmen felt like running for shelter whenever the mention of one was in the air.

Drawing a hand through her wind tangled Shirley Temples; she cast a tired look towards the imposing white brick house in the distance. For a moment, she revered the construction which had been in her family since slavery. She then headed in the opposite direction toward the lush fields where the horses grazed.

Carmen smirked. Horses. What a life her family led. So many people envied what they had- that a black family could boast such trappings.

She shivered delightfully at her quiet use of the word she'd just come across while reading a news article the week before. It was such a fitting word. All the beauty and elegance had certainly trapped her family- some of them more horrifically than others.

Wild laughter caught her ears when she neared one of the stables. Her thoughts on family and trappings cleared as curiosity set in. On softer steps, she ventured nearer towards the sturdy structure.

The laughter was sparse, but never lost its wild intensity. Carmen cast a quick look across her shoulder. Satisfied that she was alone, she took a closer look and gasped at what she saw.

Marcus Ramsey smiled his approval and settled back more comfortably against the tufts of hay lining the stall. To the casual onlooker it would have appeared that he was simply relaxing. But nothing was ever quite what it appeared where Marc was concerned. He smirked and looked down at the young woman draped across his lap. Closing his eyes, he enjoyed her dazzling oral treat and lost his hand in her hair.

He squeezed his fingers in her thick tresses when she would have pulled back for air.

"Stay on it," his voice was soft yet the intent was crude.

Roselle Simon didn't seem to mind and whispered her own sultry taunts while following Marc's orders.

Clearly, the couple was involved in the act and; for a time, oblivious to all else. That is, until Marc opened his eyes and looked directly at his younger sister.

Carmen blinked, wanting to look away but unable to. Running was out of the question as well for she couldn't move. Their gazes held. Then, in a purely lurid manner, Marc licked his lips and beckoned her forward with a wave.

Heart lurching to her chest, Carmen jerked away from the stable opening and raced away.

Marcus remained calmed. Instead of panic, Carmen's discovery had sent a rush of sensation through him. The feeling was so intense that he released his need. Roselle of course took full credit for the reaction even when Marc pushed her aside.

"Run along now before Daniel and Martha start to worry."

"Bastard," Roselle hissed, lying half naked amidst the hay. Her mouth glistened with tell-tale moisture.

Marc grinned and smoothly fixed his clothes. Thankfully, Roselle made quick work of leaving and; alone, Marc let his thoughts drift back to his sister watching as he was pleasured.

Carmen was running like the devil was at her back. The chiffon skirts of her dress rivaled the rustling sound the leaves made as she raced back toward the party.

'The devil' however was more of a figurative term just then. After all, she'd bet her brother was still on his back and being treated by the Simon spinster she'd caught him with.

In truth, 'the devil' in that instance referred to the surge of fear Marcus instilled whenever he looked her way. When she saw him moments ago, that fear had been amplified. Carmen was so muddled in her thoughts that she screamed when her running brought her up against a warm, solid wall of flesh.

Jasper Stone smiled, though concern was etched in his deep brown eyes.

"Hey? Carmen? Carmen?" He took her shoulders in a gentle hold noticing the terror on her face when they'd collided. "It's Jasper, you're okay…"

Melting then, Carmen lay against him and took time to catch her breath.

Jasper was bending to look directly into her face. "What is it? What's wrong?"

The soft coaxing tone of his voice only made her shiver more deeply. Her fingers curled like talons into his black dress shirt and she shook her head.

"Alright then, let's get you home."

"No!" She shivered then as though the idea of "home" repulsed her. "Stay with me? Stay with me here?" Without a care for her dress, she sat in the grassy clearing.

As it was a mild Savannah afternoon and full of festivity, Jasper didn't see the harm in spending a few minutes with the youngest Ramsey daughter. It was no surprise though that those 'few minutes' stirred needs that were best left alone.

Carmen Moiselle Ramsey was only thirteen- young but already portioned into the stunning woman she would become. The face of a heart stopping beauty was developing daily. Her soft easy manner mirrored the look in her alluring dark stare. Scores of young suitors had already found their way to her door.

"Do you feel like talkin', Carm?" Jasper asked when the silence sent his thoughts too far in the wrong direction.

"You deserve better than that Rose Simon."

Clearly stunned, Jasper blinked owlishly at Carmen's hissed advice. "Why?" Was all he'd dare ask.

"You're so handsome and sweet. You really care about what a girl says when she opens her mouth- not just whether her mouth could adequately accommodate your cock."

Of course he cared about what a girl had to say. Just then however, Carmen's attempt at flattery simply had him imagining things involving her that he could be killed for.

"We need to head back." He stood and expelled a sigh of relief when she followed suit.

Carmen took Jasper's arm, but squeezed in a warning manner before he could take a step.

"Watch my brother. Don't ever trust him."

Jasper watched her walk on ahead. He didn't need her to clarify which brother for he knew without a doubt that it was Marcus.

***

"Thank you, Dora." Marcella Ramsey smiled up at the lovely dark woman who'd placed a glass of iced tea to the woven end table. The cool observation returned to her slate gray stare when the young maid walked off. "Has Westin done anything?" She asked, turning back to watch Sybil Deas.

"Oh no, no Marcella- nothing like that." The woman shook her head. "Westin is a wonderful boy- handsome, smart, mannerly- did I say how handsome he is?"

Laughter resonated between the two friends. It wasn't long though, before concern returned to dull the usual sparkle in Sybil's light hazel eyes.

"The kids are in their twenties Marcy," Sybil began to wring her lace-gloved hands. "Westin's yet to propose and-" she glanced across her shoulder, "and I'm certain the two of them are having relations- sexual relations. Now, Elton may be too nervous to say anything but that's not the case between us, is it?" Sybil straightened a bit while questioning her old friend.

Marcella appeared skeptical. "I'm sure if Elton felt concern he would've said something to Quent by now- they've been friends as long as we have."

"Yes, but Quentin *is* Elton's boss." Sybil cleared her throat. "There's only so much he'd say about something like that and you know how men can be. But you and I-" She reached for her tea glass and tilted it toward Marcella. "We go way back and I don't feel a bit shy about bringing this up. I have to look out for my daughter's future. Having your own daughters, I'm sure you can understand that." Losing her taste for the tea, Sybil set aside the glass and fisted her hands in her lap. "I don't want Bris giving up her goodies with no commitments."

Marcella bristled beneath the fabric of her cream linen dress. She felt no anger towards her friend's perceptions however. Eyes crinkling when she smiled, Marcella leaned over to pat Sybil's clenched hands. "I understand where you're coming from girl, but… from what I've been told by my son, it's Briselle who's shunning commitment in return for her… goodies."

Sybil gasped and then looked around quickly to see whether anyone strolling the wide back porch had heard her outburst. "What are you saying?"

"Sweetie Westin's been proposing for years only to have Briselle turn him down every time."

Stunned, Sybil Deas could only stare open-mouthed at her dearest friend.

At that moment, Briselle Deas was in fact turning down another proposal from her boyfriend of nine years. Lying upon a sea of hay, she stared at the gleaming diamond positioned inside its black velvet box.

"Westin why-"

"Just stop, Bri. Stop. You know what this is and you damn well know why."

Briselle rolled her eyes and tried to sit up. Westin stopped her by smothering her slight form with his lanky, muscular one.

"This isn't going to happen."

She spoke in that soft, breathy tone that never failed to arouse him. Whatever else she was preparing to say was effectively silenced when he thrust his tongue inside her mouth.

Of course, Bri couldn't resist. She'd never been able to resist him and snuggled deeper into their embrace. Boldly, she thrust her tongue eagerly against his. A delicious interlude surfaced and; in seconds, the bodice of her demure white frock was open and his handsome face was nestled between her small, full breasts.

Keeping one hand secure about Briselle's wrists, Westin feasted on her firming nipples until he heard her pleading for him to do more. Stopping then, he raised his head.

"Do you really think I'd ever let you go, Bri?"

"Why?" She stiffened and the affect was mirrored on her delicate features. "Why West? Because I'll lift my skirt and drop my panties for you anytime you ask? You could get any girl at this cotillion to do the same."

"But do you really believe I could stand you not being mine?" Softly enraged then, his sleek brows drew close. "Do you think I could function knowing someone else could have you?"

She looked away then as tears pooled her eyes. Covering her face, she quietly willed them away.

"Baby…" West felt on the verge of tears himself.

"Don't," she shook her head and moved to pull her dress together. "We've been going steady nine years West and I've lost two babies already."

"Bri-"

"No. Please West. I've lost *two*." She let him see her wet face. "What does that mean?"

He cupped her chin. "It means we keep trying."

She wrenched her chin from his fingers. "We aren't even married. Now, maybe that's why or maybe it's because it'll never be meant for us to have a child. I can't let you-"

"What? Love you. Love *only* you?"

She sucked her teeth. "You know what I'm saying."

"And what *I'm* saying is I love you and that means more to me than anything- *anything* Bri." He kissed fresh tears from her eyes and tugged her into a crushing embrace.

***

"Daniel!" Quentin Ramsey's voice bellowed above the mingled conversation and laughter energizing the party. He extended hands toward local carpenter Daniel Simon and his wife Martha.

The two men had maintained an easy relationship over the years despite the fact that Daniel had declined Quentin's numerous requests that he dissolve his successful carpentry business and come head his own team at Ramsey.

"Glad you're here and with all these lovelies." Quent teased the dark towering man and then nodded towards Martha and the couple's four daughters.

"Thanks so much for inviting us, Quentin." Martha Simon's honey gaze rivaled the tone of her skin for radiance as she took in the scope of the event and the guests dressed in their finest attire.

Quentin shrugged. "I'll keep trying to win y'all over anyway I can 'til Dan comes to work for Ramsey."

"Precisely why I'll never come over," Daniel's words always carried on a chuckle. "I'd be a fool to give up this kind of bribery!"

As the trio laughed merrily, Marcus Ramsey strolled up to greet his father's guests and their daughters. The girls stood behind their parents and smiled graciously. Like the dutiful and respectful son, Marc greeted the Simons- with special charming attention reserved for the daughters.

The three eldest made no secret of their soft spots for the Ramsey's dashing, second son. Roselle Simon in particular braced back her shoulders and held her head a smidge higher in expectation of a special greeting from Marc. The expectancy in her wide browns dimmed noticeably when he offered no such sweetness in light of the intimacies they'd just shared. Her mood quickly improved though when he spared her a sly wink.

Surprisingly, no one noticed Marc's expression sharpen with intense interest when his dark gaze settled on the caramel-toned beauty that stood a foot shorter than her robust sisters. Marcus moved on before anyone noticed the look he spent on eighteen year old Josephine Ramsey. Josephine certainly didn't notice, for she'd kept her eyes downcast when the gorgeous Ramsey approached.

***

Boisterous laughter filled the gazebo. The five young women there enjoyed delicious cool cider, the delights of the day and the bawdy yet amusing comments of their often times naughty girlfriend.

Georgia Ramsey made the act of tucking a lock of wavy hair behind an ear; the most seductively glamorous move one could muster without breaking a sweat. Georgia's four friends envied and loved her as much as they feared and disliked her. The girl's allure was intriguing to say the least. She could cut down a friend and build them up in one breath.

It was a difficult thing for one to tell whether Georgia Ramsey was being honest or cruel when she struck out with her words. To Georgia, honesty and cruelty were one in the same as people could rarely accept the truth when it was spoken in reference to them.

"You better keep it down before our mothers get a whiff of what we're discussing." Priscilla Dartmouth scolded her friend.

"Fuck it; they know what we talk about. They talk about it themselves." Georgia inspected her fresh manicure. "My Mama knew the very day I gave it up to Felix. She said I was walkin' different."

The laughter rose to a voluminous roar.

"But that's not so bad Georgia," Greta Weeks was saying before the laughter totally faded. "You and Felix been together for years. Hell, it's almost like you're sleepin' with your husband."

"*Almost*," Georgia appeared to shudder. "And *almost* is all it'll ever be unless that nigga got some money and prospects in his future."

"Well Mr. Q would see to that, right?" Melody Brown asked in reference to Quentin Ramsey.

"I'd hope so," Georgia came down a little. "Felix ain't interested in 'hand me down success'- that's what he calls it. Talkin' 'bout he's tryin' to make it on his own."

"Well that's commendable girl." Denise Orey raved.

Georgia sucked her teeth and focused on her other manicured hand. "Probably," she sighed, "but that still leaves him bein' a broke nigga and I need a man who'll keep me livin' like my daddy meant for me to."

"Well why are you with Felix, then?" Priscilla smoothed a hand across her chignon, hoping to downplay her interest in the matter. "I mean, I know tons of girls who'd love a chance with his fine ass."

"I'm with him because his *fine ass* is *damn good* in bed." Georgia's smile was cool and deadly while adding a sharper loveliness to her pecan brown face. "In light of that, I'll just be keeping him for a while."

The boisterous laughter rose once more.

***

Fifteen year old Catrina Jeffries forgot her station for a moment and indulged in a few moments of fantasizing. She tapped her sneaker shod foot to the Isley Brother's *"Shout"* and imagined she was one of the beautiful girls floating about the grounds of the Ramsey estate in a heart stopping dress of silk and chiffon.

One day, she promised herself. One day she'd be president of Jeffries Catering. By then, her parent's business would have branched out to include conferences and banquets in addition to birthday parties and cotillions. She'd see to it. Then, she'd waltz into a gathering like this- a self made woman. Everyone would whisper that she was the smart, lovely president of the most successful catering company in the whole state.

"Catrina Marie! That tub ain't gon' empty itself!"

"'Kay Mama!" Catrina rolled her eyes. Just then, she'd have to accept her current post as fat dumper. She glared distastefully at the vat of fish grease she'd been sent to dispose of.

Casting off her images of grandeur, Catrina took a moment to gather stray tendrils that had fallen loose of her ponytail. She whipped the heavy tresses into a fresh knot and was checking the tightness of her rubber band when she turned to find herself staring at another fantasy.

She studied the boy who studied her. Tall; with deep set eyes dark as night, he was a thing to be swooned over. Catrina found herself celebrating her luck at viewing such a beautiful thing. At the same time she cursed her luck for viewing such a beautiful thing while he viewed her with splatters of fish and chicken fat on her faded pedal pushers and the light blue T-shirt graced with the name JEFFERIES CATERERS in black velvet letters.

"Catrina Marie! Don't make me come back there, girl! Get them vats emptied and get back up here!"

Lashes fluttering, Catrina willed her beloved mother be stricken with a momentary bout of laryngitis.

"Comin' Mama!" She started to turn when she heard him ask if she needed help.

"Thank you, but no." Catrina celebrated the fact that her voice hadn't deserted her.

Damon Ramsey nodded and silently ordered himself to stop gawking at the beauty that'd rendered him immobile.

Made in the USA
Lexington, KY
24 November 2010